# T̶H̶E̶ ̶F̶L̶I̶G̶H̶T̶
# OF THE
# BARBAROUS RELIC

## GEORGE FORD SMITH

What follows is a work of fiction.  Though references are made to historical and contemporary figures, the characters themselves are invented, and any resemblance they may have to actual persons is purely coincidental.

To
My family – here, there, and everywhere

## PROLOG

The man approaching him in the August twilight was tall and thick through the chest, though nothing in his movements suggested a threat. He strolled with a hand slipped casually in his pants pocket, even stopping once to pick up a piece of litter and toss it in a nearby barrel. He could almost pass for one of D.C.'s tourists taking a late walk through a public park.

Yet, on seeing him Ricky Sawyer's stomach churned. This was no casual meeting taking place. He had known this moment would come and had dreaded it, and Sawyer was not prone to unnecessary fears. As he waited under one of the many security lights in the area, the man stopped abruptly in the shadows, kneeled down and retied a running shoe that was properly laced. Sawyer took the hint and moved all 282 pounds of himself over to join him.

"What's with the cloak and dagger?" Sawyer asked.

The man stood up. "I need the favor returned."

Sawyer chuckled nervously. "What do you want me to do? Hack the president's PC?"

"Nothing that easy, my friend. I need you to set up a website. Over time, you'll be supplied with content. But I need the site established now, to make sure the name is available."

"You could go to anyone for a website."

"Not this one."

Sawyer hesitated. "What's going on?"

"How much do you remember from Professor Stefanelli's class?"

"Everything. Paper versus rock. Paper won. We lost."

"Right. I want to put an end to paper. Permanently."

Sawyer chuckled. "Sounds like you're going to blow up your office."

"More along the lines of a crash course in hoax awareness. That's why I need your help."

"Where's the danger come in?"

"The content. The power holders won't like it."

"There are a lot of things they don't like. Why—"

"—I guarantee this will upset them beyond anything you can imagine. You'll have to keep a low profile. Make that no profile. You'll have to disappear."

"Tall order for a whale, chief."

"Any taller than breaking into the Eccles Building network?"

"No, guess not."

"I think you'll be okay. But listen, this won't work unless you understand what's at stake. Do you?"

Sawyer thought for a moment. "Yeah. Civilization. Under paper, little guys like me lose their wealth, liberty, and sometimes their lives, while government grows more bloated, corrupt, and oppressive."

"And the cause?"

"Paper. Inflation."

"What's inflation done for us historically?"

"According to Professor Stefanelli, without inflation we have no World War I, no Great Depression, no World War II, no Cold War, no Viet Nam, no taxpayer-funded bailouts, no bubbles, no war on terrorism, no Iraq. Without inflation Cindy Sheehan is just another mom with a son. Without inflation, instead of endless acres of white crosses marking the battlefield dead, men are left free to live. Imagine that. And when those men are geniuses like me or Google founders Page and Brin, the whole world profits. Without inflation to build up militaries, we might've had nuclear power without nuclear bombs. She also said something to the effect that if inflation were a disease, it would be considered the number one killer of human life. There was more. Give me time and I'll remember it."

"Do you agree with any of that?"

"Too simplistic. But then, where would the computer age be without electricity? Pull the plug and the computers go away. So it was hard to argue with her."

"But you did."

"Of course. But the truth is, without massive amounts of money the First World War doesn't go far – four months, according to a writer who was around at the time. And nothing beats the printing press for producing large amounts of money in a hurry – paper money. And if World War I is aborted, the rest of the century looks a little brighter. I would say she's not far from the truth, at least."

"Not bad for a hacker. You talked about inflation but didn't define it. Can you?"

"Paper."

"More precisely . . ."

"I didn't expect a quiz. The going definition is a rise in the general price level."

"Do you accept that definition?"

"No, because you can have inflation without price increases. Productivity improvements work against rising prices."

"Any other reason not to accept the definition of inflation as rising prices?"

"Yeah, it obscures the cause."

"Which is?"

"More paper. More money. An increase in the money supply."

"How is the money supply increased?"

"Through treachery. First the snap," Sawyer said, snapping his fingers, "in which the Fed creates money from nothing. Then the crank," he continued, rotating his right arm in a cranking motion, "as the banks multiply that amount through credit expansion. Then the pop" – He slapped his hands – "when the bubble bursts and everyone gets fired. Sawyer's theory of the business cycle in three words: snap, crankle, and pop."

"But isn't that how prosperity is funded? By increasing the money supply?"

"No. That's how the inflationary boom is started or prolonged."

"Is that a good thing?"

"It is if you're one of the insiders. Without it, the military/industrial/ congressional/welfare racket takes a big hit. Governments would have to rely mostly on taxes to pay their bills."

"What would that do for war if governments had to pay for it with taxes?"

"Make it an endangered species."

"So if you're a government bent on war—"

"Inflation is a sacred cow."

"And who causes inflation?"

"Who?"

"Yes."

"I'm looking at him."

"I think you understand what we're fighting."

"I do."

They shook hands.

"I'll be in touch," the man said.


Later that night Sawyer received an email containing a web address only. After confirming the site didn't exist he set about to create it, as agreed.

In the weeks that followed, Sawyer would find it difficult to believe their conversation was at all serious. Nothing had been added to the website, and other than the terse email there had been no contact between them. The topic they had discussed seemed weird at the time and even more so as time passed. Perhaps their meeting was a brutal prank, a form of payback for the hack he had pulled. It seemed like it was. He began to feel like a fool for trusting him.

But Sawyer was wrong. The day finally arrived when all doubts were forever removed.

**1**

Preston Mathews wiped his brow and tried to ignore the rumbling in the distant sky.

Now 51, he was engaged in a long-shot undertaking that was for him a rare instance of honest labor, even though it entailed such sterling qualities as theft, deception, and willful destruction – and probably worse, if you counted what it would bring in its wake.

This part of the project – turning the front of his barn into a billboard – had tested his patience for the last three months while he took care of his professional life. It had put him at odds with tape, templates, subtle hues of paint, bugs, foul weather, and nosy neighbors. But the phrase *labor of love* was something he could sing from his heart now.

Mathews had been detailing his barn with the likeness of the product he managed, a mass-produced item popular the world over. His painting resembled the product in every respect but one.

And he was about to tell the world what that one difference meant.

He was kneeling on a scaffold supported by charred burn barrels, applying the paint with a turbine-powered spray gun. Flecks of paint gave his black hair a prematurely gray look. A respirator covered his nose and mouth, and soft cotton gloves pampered his hands. With a flick of his finger he gunned the paint onto the barn surface, using the High-Volume Low-Pressure applicator in non-bleeder mode for better rendering of detail.

Thunder came again suddenly, this time directly overhead, but it was only the owl beating its great wings as it landed in an opening near the peak of the barn. Mathews stood and leaned back from his waist, stretching his muscles. He watched the ghostly predator peering out at fields of withered corn and perhaps the shoreline of the pond, waiting for the right movement that would signal food.

"Hope you like your new home, Chief," Mathews called out, his words muffled by his respirator. The owl twisted its neck to gaze down at him, its heart-shaped pale physiognomy looking like a mask of its own, worn perhaps to terrify its prey. "This one won't be around much longer," he said quietly. "A day, maybe. Maybe less."

His old friend flew down to him, and Mathews offered it a gloved hand. It perched there about two feet from his face, its talons a sharp reminder that he needed better protection. "You suffer from chronic insomnia or are your nocturnal wires just crossed? Either way, I can't help you . . . I've got work to do, buddy. Can't stand here chatting, especially with these gloves." He raised his arm to launch the bird into flight but it refused to move. "Come on, it's time to break with the past. Up, up!" As if understanding his command, the owl unfolded its wings and flew back to the loft. Mathews dropped to one knee and went back to work.

He was about to beat a self-imposed deadline, leaving him plenty of time to be in the air before dark. And he hoped something – the approaching storm, perhaps – would scare his little friend away by then.

When the last of the paint was on the barn he ripped his mask off and flung it over his shoulder. He hopped off the scaffold and backed away haltingly, unable to tear his eyes from his work. Even at six-foot-three he had needed his ten-foot Husky stepladder for the upper regions of the image. He wanted the picture to be imposing, yet connected to Americana. A barn ad was the answer.

He kept easing away from the image until he reached a white-rail fence about thirty yards distant. He laughed. "Not bad for an unskilled laborer," he said aloud. "If only Mount Rushmore had a sculpture like this."

He grabbed his hi-res Samsung from a nearby fence post and took a few pictures. The owl remained poised above his masterpiece like a lookout on an old ship. "It's a work of art, Chief!" Mathews shouted. Then quietly, as he faded into thought: "An unmoved mover... We'll see, won't we?"

He recalled reading about Harley Warrick, who spent 55 years of his life painting MAIL POUCH chewing tobacco ads on some 22,000 barns across Appalachia and the Midwest. The government finally put him out of business by banning outside tobacco advertising. He tried to imagine government's reaction if copies of his image adorned the roofs and sides of the country's barns.

Or their reaction to just one barn – a certain barn in eastern Virginia.

## 2

Mathews stepped out of his '76 Ford Ranger at the Cedar Airfield parking lot, tucked a bulging duffle bag under his arm and made a dash for the office some fifty yards distant. With his plain black sweatshirt, old jeans, and paint-streaked running shoes, he almost looked like the second shift janitorial help arriving late. There was nothing janitorial about his stride, though, which was still remarkably graceful in spite of the gravel surface. The airfield itself was a two-runway hybrid affair, with most of its acreage devoted to cedar tree farming, the chief component of its paltry revenue.

As he arrived at the door, Mathews thought briefly of the remark Nina made years ago about his running style being so athletic, adding that it had been wasted on an academic. Given that she had nerd qualities herself, her remark had to be heavily discounted, but it was still comforting to think that *just maybe* some part of his high school quarterbacking days were still in evidence. How easily the good memories came, with a fateful flight looming.

"Greetings, men," he called out to the two attendants as he came into the office. He immediately began filling out a log book at the counter. The attendants had been killing the remainder of their day talking about a possible UVA upset of Michigan State tomorrow at Spartan Stadium. Seeing Mathews put ink to the log doused all talk of football.

"Happy Halloween, Dr. Mathews," Wes Sutherland said a little too cheerfully.

"Hey," Mathews replied absentmindedly without looking at him.

Sutherland was in his early forties and lean as a blade. His younger and beefier coworker Ed Ramsey was too dumbstruck to speak. Sutherland's mouth hung open as he watched Mathews finish his entry.

"How are you, sir?" Sutherland asked.

Mathews set the pen down. "Almost perfect, Wes. Almost perfect. Know what that's like?"

"Not without a hangover trailin' after it. Dr. Mathews—"

"Ever race a train at a railroad crossing?"

"No, sir, I haven't."

"Neither have I. Don't ever plan to. But this storm coming in will be pretty close. Can I get a flight in before it hits? Yeah, I think so."

"The storm could be here any minute, Dr. Mathews. You're not serious, are you?"

"Never been more serious in my life."

"You're also betting your life, sir."

"Then I better get moving."

Mathews turned and went back outside.

Several minutes passed before Sutherland and Ramsey decided they really ought to be more insistent. They hustled outside past an arch-roofed hangar to the spacious shanty where Mathews kept his personal airship, a harvest gold 1941 Waco ("Wah-Ko") UPF-7 biplane. What could be worse than seeing a man fly an old relic into a storm? Seeing him nonchalantly spray-paint it first.

They had stopped just inside the hanger and stood watching him alternate between shaking a paint can then spraying black letters on the back of the fuselage. He went about it in cavalier fashion, like a vandal scrawling graffiti.

He turned and saw them. "Think long shelf life, men! Things that people will always want. Grand pianos, fine jewelry. Gold! If you have a good place to hide it. Don't store it in a goddamn bank." Then he stepped back to look at his lettering. "How 'bout it, guys? Catchy?"

They were too dumbstruck to speak.

Mathews went on. "And don't tell anyone you own it. No one, not even your mothers. If some nosy bureaucrat inquires about a sudden depletion of your cash holdings, make something up. Tell him you blew it at Vegas, but don't tell him you bought physical gold. They will take it from you, if not now, someday."

He frowned at the lettering on his biplane. "I hope I spelled 'barbarous' right. Oh, damn! Hang on." He stepped to the rear cockpit and reached down inside it. When he turned back he was holding two bundles of money bound with mustard-colored straps. He threw one to each man as if tossing peanuts to squirrels. "Some advisor I am! Tell you what to buy but leave you empty-handed."

The two men looked at the wad of money in their hands with complete idiocy. Then they stared at each other, their eyes seeming to spread across their faces. Sutherland stuck a hand in Ramsey's chest: "Go back and call nine-one-one. I'll try to hold him." He had to shove Ramsey to get him moving.

Mathews was pushing the plane out of the hanger from the right side of the rear cockpit when Sutherland came up to him.

"Dr. Mathews, I can't let you do this. Something's not right."

Mathews kept working. "I know. That's why I've got to do it."

"I mean with you, sir. You're not yourself today. Why don't you ride this storm out with us? I'll put on a fresh pot of coffee."

"Any other time I'd love nothing better. Give me a hand here, will you?"

Wes shook his head. "Sir, I can't. It's - it's suicide. If I let you go I'll get shot a hundred times over. And I couldn't blame them."

Mathews stopped, slapped the fuselage and let out a long sigh. "You're a good man, Wes." He moved over to Sutherland and dropped a hand on his shoulder. "I need you to listen very carefully."

"Yes, sir."

"I'm not going up in the air to get my kicks challenging Mother Nature. If I were, your case against my sanity would be unassailable. You might say I'm challenging human nature, but without details that's just empty rhetoric. So let's just say this is a mission, a very critical mission." He removed his hand and stood back. "Now, tell me what you just heard me say."

"I heard you say . . . the hell with the weather, you're going on a very critical mission."

"Well put. Think Paul Revere, okay? In a loose sense. Right now, I need you to help me get started." Sutherland looked scared to death. "Now what's the problem?"

He held the money up. "*This.*"

"Consider it a tax rebate," Mathews said. "That's all I can say. If you feel uncomfortable accepting it then don't spend it. Now, let's get going. I really don't like that thunder."

"I have a young daughter to support, Dr. Mathews. She depends on me."

Mathews yanked a bill from Sutherland's cache of loot and scrawled a note on it, his hand racing, using the fuselage for support. Watching Cedar's most distinguished client scribble a message on one of the banknotes didn't help Sutherland breathe any easier. When Mathews finished he held it up to the attendant's face.

Sutherland struggled with the handwriting. "This cer . . . certifies—"

"— 'This certifies that Wes Sutherland made a conscientious effort to stop me, Preston Mathews, from taking off with a God-awful thunderstorm approaching.' You're covered." He stuffed the note in Sutherland's hand. "Krista won't miss any meals. Now, let's get moving."

Sutherland looked at the note, then cast a pleading glance about the hangar. "God help us."

"Oh! One more thing," Mathews said, heading for the rear cockpit again.

Moments later Ramsey came rushing into the hanger and stopped. Sutherland was holding a camera to his face taking aim at Mathews, who was standing next to the inscription on the back of the fuselage. Mathews smiled like a proud papa.

"I made the call," Ramsey said.

Southerland lowered the camera to his chest and looked at his co-worker with tortured eyes. "Call them back," he said.

3

The wind cut through him, had he bothered to notice.

He was flying from an open cockpit in the rear of the plane, with a heavy tarp stretched over the seat in front. He had added aviator goggles and a white scarf to his attire. The wind had picked up, and he could feel the double-winger straining under the control stick. The struts and wires shook and howled. Sixty weight oil from the 220 hp Continental 670 engine was forming a faint film on his windscreen. Need new gaskets, he concluded, and laughed at his own dark humor. His venerable Waco had no business dueling with thunderstorms.

Morrisville was only a few miles distant but it meant flying into one massive cumulonimbus formation to get there. He kept his airspeed at 110 mph, his altitude at 200 feet. The duffle bag squeezed between his legs and seat felt reassuring, but visions of disaster played in his mind.

For one thing, he had never flown in foul weather. He imagined coming in low and catching a sudden crosswind that would send him spinning into a pasture nose-first. And he could only hope it would be a pasture; he would be mostly buzzing a town, with houses and children and cars. Thumbing his nose at a storm was the kind of hubris the gods love to punish. He could end up in ashes before he even reached Morrisville, turning his trip into a fool's final errand.

But even if he survived Morrisville, there was still a more critical jaunt to make.

The town rolled toward him, the dark sky looming behind it like the shadow of an avenging giant. He brought the plane down lower and dropped his speed until he could read road signs. He was coming up on Main Street. He was so low he was almost part of the scant road traffic, a moving violation with two wings. He loafed by the town's Arby's then the lone KFC. Two boys were helping their dad pump gas at an antediluvian BP station, and he circled leisurely around it, wanting people to notice him. One of the kids appeared to shout and mimed shooting a bow and arrow at him. Some weapon. Biplanes get no respect.

He passed over a little church and graveyard on the north side of town, then made a grand sweep over a farm and came back for a second pass. The storm had turned the world black, and wind rocked his plane like a dingy in a gale. Lightning lit up the buildings and houses ahead, and got his heart racing. Then the rain hit, turning his cockpit into a cistern, and a world of limited detail suddenly disappeared. His cockpit was filling up. He imagined the ultimate folly – not crashing, but *sinking*.

He looked down. Rooftops and trees passed under him, then something suggesting the tarmac of the BP station. More bodies had joined the dad and his sons. He thought he could make out the fast food joints. A storm of this intensity usually cleared the roads, but two cars were moving right along a little behind him. Were they hoping to catch a view of the inevitable? Hell, yes. Why else would Morrisville send high-speed reconnaissance out in weather like this? Had to be a fool up there, and sure as heck there's money to be gotten. Be there with a camera when he crashes and make yourself a good buck. Wes Sutherland could join the act too, with a photo showing off the bill Mathews signed, which he could post for a ransom on eBay, assuming the government didn't confiscate it first.

As suddenly as it had arrived the deluge disappeared and became a drizzle, and the world began to take on shapes with hard edges. Ahead of him was the most beautiful landing strip he had ever seen – the highway he had followed coming into town. He would set the *Barbarous Relic* down there, get out and hug the earth.

That's what he desperately wanted to do. He circled back into the storm cell instead.

There was nothing like a madman to draw a crowd's attention, or a town's, and the storm was an unexpected asset if it didn't kill him. The wind buffeted him, and now the rain was turning white and bouncing. He was being pummeled with frozen balls of ice. Not to be distracted he reached down and grabbed bunches of strapped hundred-dollar-bills from his duffle bag. And of course he forgot to remove the damn straps and immediately put his teeth to work tearing them off.  He flung the bills over the side.  Along with the hail, Morrisville was being bathed in a classic handout to a certain few, who would naturally use their good tidings to fertilize the global economy.

"By the power vested in me," he screamed into the maelstrom, "I hereby anoint you privileged insiders, Morrisville!  Come and get it!"

He weaved as best he could through town, leaving a trail of Franklin-faced notes fluttering behind him, then swung out over the farm on the other end of Morrisville and laid some Fed fairy dust on it.  A small funnel cloud was coming up on him as he moved across the farmer's field.  His heart hammered in his chest.  He had never seen a twister before, except in the movies.  He gave it a wide berth and doubled back for another pass through town, marveling at his relic's stubborn refusal to disintegrate.  "Twisters and greenbacks, folks – a double whammy!"

He wished mightily he could watch them as they gathered up their loot.  But he had promises to keep . . .

He finished his second S-turn through town and exited the womb of the storm.  Without prelude or ceremony he found himself on the final leg of the trip, the part most critical to his plan.

He had flown this course nine days earlier on a sun-drenched fall day and had flown it many times before then.  Nine days ago his intestines rebelled thinking about these next few minutes.  He had done the calculations.  He knew what airspeed, altitude, and angle of approach he would need.

Those were the known quantities. What bothered him was the unknown, for which his instruments were of no use.

Everything had seemed so clear last night and earlier today. If his conscience had tapped him on the shoulder and asked him what the hell he was doing with all this barn business and the biplane, he would've had an articulate answer. He could say he wanted a different world than the one he lived in and was one of the few people who could possibly start the painful process of reshaping it. But that was last night's answer. Now, with his life spinning on a roulette wheel, he couldn't produce a single goddamn reason why he was in this flimsy aircraft. All he could think of was the unreal task ahead of him and how he might talk himself out of it. Rationalization was the only thing that might save him.

But was it really wrong to consider the fabulous life he was giving up? And for who, exactly, was he throwing it all away? Most Americans didn't care about this issue and nothing he could do would make them care. They're busy with their kids' soccer team or struggling with another plumbing leak – don't bother them with esoteric exercises. The big shots didn't want some idiotic boat-rocker threatening their revenue stream. Don't tell them about truth – truth is what keeps them on top and gets their kids into the snottier schools.

No, this idea he was pursuing might be seriously flawed. If he goes through with it, politicians and talking heads will cast pity on him for having caved to the stress of his office. The simple messages he would be leaving could never overcome generations of carefully delivered indoctrination. His plan was futile. Where was his incentive? Had he forgotten everything he knew about economics? He needed to turn his plane around.

His farm rolled into view, a terrifying sight. He never imagined his peaceful little spread could inspire so much fear. Where other men of his means might have bought a villa in some exotic locale to complement their rural estate or urban suite, he throws down his cash on an attention-deprived 27-acre corn farm with a resident owl. It made perfect sense at the time. Now it seemed more like a funny farm, reflecting the character of its owner.

He should be back at the airfield having coffee with the guys. They didn't want him to do this. Who the hell are you to do it for them?

He slowed and came in low, the wheels almost skimming the pond and a few stray stalks of corn. The barn's graven image rose in his face. His masterpiece, his gift to the world, destined to be destroyed. *You're not yourself today, Dr. Mathews. And this barn of yours – Jesus Christ, what have you done?!* He laughed and *vroomed* over it.

Chief, he had noticed, was still resting on his perch at the top of the barn. He never budged, didn't take off flying like a smart bird would when the plane roared past, probably because he knew the pilot so well. Maybe he stayed to make sure Mathews didn't chicken out.

He circled back for a second approach to the barn, swinging past a stand of yellow pines. The barn was headed straight for him, growing bigger. The bottom fell out of his stomach.

His only impulse was to scream. Yet somewhere in his mind was a little procedure he had to follow. If he came up short on nerve now—

Preston Vincent Mathews screamed.

4

On a small farm outside Morrisville, 15-year-old Lisa Beeman indulged in fantasies of Hollywood as she pulled the laces loose on her running shoes. She sat on the threshold of the doorway of her father's side porch with the door swung open behind her, having just spent a frenzied half hour running around a muddy field in shorts. She had left her father snoring on a recliner, and with luck he would still be that way when she slipped back inside. Certainly no noise she could make would wake him.

She didn't think much about where the money might have come from. Maybe it was stolen, and the thief was ditching it before he got caught. Maybe the same breeze that passed over their long gravel drive and left two white ash uprooted and a Sears 21″ power mower relocated to a horseshoe pit helped itself to a little cash from his cockpit. Whatever -- she didn't care. She had a blouse-full of hundred dollar bills, enough to get her heart pumping about the Big Screen.

She pulled her shoes off and zipped up her windbreaker. If anyone should ask, the damage outside was minor. In time the ash would make good firewood, and the Sears had long been rummage sale material.

Soon she would be calling on ad agencies and asking for auditions to do TV commercials. She could live frugally on her fortuitous find. Commercials would be big, but they were only a step.

She stood up, her heart-stopping good looks still conspicuous after a whirlwind trip around the field.

She started to go inside when something on the horizon to her right turned her head.

Miles off, rising above the pines from the other side of a distant hill, she could see faint spirals of smoke.

*Lightning fire*, she guessed, and slipped inside.

5

By 12:30 a.m. that night Maxwell Woodrow Gage, President of the United States, was stretched out on a couch in the Oval Office with a cold cloth over his eyes, doctoring his latest migraine.

He had been counting on golf trips to Annapolis, West Point, and Colorado Springs over the weekend to relieve the stress of a week fighting party leaders over two off-budget wars. Now he waited in agony with three advisors, one of whom was on the phone getting the latest report from Podunk, Virginia. The lights were so low it looked like a romantic tryst instead of an emergency meeting.

Mel Stewart, the advisor on the line, paced the room nodding and asking questions. He had been a lineman at Rutgers and had been with Gage since Max's first senate race eighteen years earlier in Connecticut. Gage liked him because he had enough modesty to temper his ambition and lacked the wits to pull an Ides of March. His advice was charmingly credulous -- straight out of a Boy Scout handbook -- but his loyalty and work ethic were priceless.

The news Stewart was getting had him scratching the back of his neck so hard it was turning the skin red raw. Normally, the call would have been on speaker, but Gage was in no condition to listen to a squawking female voice trying to talk over the crisis workers behind her.

"Yeah, keep us posted," Stewart said, ending the call. He turned to the others and let out a tense breath of air.

"The plane that went down on Mathews' farm has been confirmed as Mathews' biplane."

"Jesus Christ," Gage moaned.

"The wreck is pretty bad. She described it as twisted metal and a pile of smoking ashes. They haven't recovered any remains yet."

"Any signs of criminal involvement?" asked Doug Foster, who sat hunched in a chair near the president. Compared to Stewart, Foster looked like a frail water boy, but he came from a family of political donors whose friendship up-and-coming politicians did well to cultivate. Foster, who held a Ph.D. in philosophy from Yale, was given to Gage as an inseparable part of the donor package.

"No criminal involvement," Stewart said to him. "However, there's evidence to suggest Mathews may have suffered . . . a personal breakdown."

"What kind of evidence?" snapped Thomas Hawkins, Gage's Chief of Staff, his shapeless bulk sprawled in a chair next to Foster. Hawkins used to play poker with Gage at Yale where the future president was in awe of Hawkins' ability to cheat at just about anything and get away with it. Hawkins, who liked to boast that he never studied, had received two honorary doctorates since leaving Yale.

"Well, of course, neither I nor Special Agent Frenzel-Johnson are qualified to issue such a judgment officially," Stewart said, moving to a laptop on a Queen Anne end table, "but Mathews' behavior was unusual, to say the least. For one thing, according to neighbors, he had been working diligently rendering an image of a dollar bill on the front of his barn. It was huge – side to side. When he wasn't around he kept it cloaked with a heavy tarp. From the looks of it, he had completed the image earlier in the day. Paint cans and sprayer gun were lying on the scaffold, which was still standing under the rendering."

"He bought that place to relax on weekends," Foster said. "It sounds like he took his job with him."

"Took his job and warped it," Stewart said. "Instead of Washington's face he painted a Jolly Roger."

Gage nearly inhaled his washcloth. He sat up wildly and gaped at Stewart.

"Special Agent Frenzel-Johnson is sending a picture," Stewart continued. "It should be here in a second." He opened the lid on the laptop, waking it up.

Stewart had almost no sense of humor, yet the words he had just uttered couldn't possibly be taken seriously. The president rose from the couch, the washcloth dangling from his hand, and searched the big man's face for some comforting sign.

"I'm afraid it's true, sir," Stewart said to Gage's unasked question.

Gage tossed the washcloth across the room and dropped down on the couch.

"What are they doing with the barn?" Hawkins demanded.

"Searching it," Stewart said.

"I'm sorry," Gage said, smiling and shaking his head, "this isn't working for me. Preston Mathews desecrated the American dollar -- on his barn -- then plowed his plane into it? Or tried to and missed? That would mean he was insane. A major nut who didn't know night from day. We're talking about a man who a few days ago was like any one of us." He looked around at his advisors. "Someone make sense of that."

"Stress," Foster said glumly.

"Any other details?" Hawkins asked Stewart.

"Several things, but . . . not sure how much help they'll be in explaining this. The guys at the hangar where Mathews kept his biplane said he took a can of black spray paint and inscribed the phrase "barbarous relic" near the tail before taking off. The color of Mathews' plane was gold.

"Also, there's a report from the nearby village of Morrisville that a biplane made several passes over the town during a bad storm. The only biplane known to be in the air was Mathews'."

"Sounds like he tried to kill himself in the storm, and when that failed he tried to kamikaze his barn and missed," Foster said. "The poor devil was stressed to the hilt."

Hawkins shot him a look of disgust. "A man sitting on top of the world in just about every respect you can think of -- ON TOP OF THE FRICKING WORLD -- decides he couldn't take it anymore and does himself in," he said. "Excuse me, but I think there's something missing."

"No, not really," Foster said. "Consider the painting. If a man comes to believe his life's work was all wrong, there may be no incentive to go on living."

"Cut the pop psyche crap," Gage said. Then to Stewart: "Anything else?"

"Yeah," Stewart said. He turned the laptop around so it faced the president. The other two leaned in to see it with him. The screen showed a photo of Mathews' barn with the edges bleeding into darkness and the visible portion -- the dollar bearing the pirate sign -- illuminated by a raging yellowish light from a nearby fire.

Gage shuddered. "It's the work of the devil."

"It's an End Times prophecy," Foster said.

A few moments of silence ensued after Stewart closed the lid on the computer and set it down. Gage looked at his advisors with sunken eyes. "Listen to me very carefully. We don't want anyone, anywhere doing forensics on the plane or the barn. Even a hint that something was kooky about his death could be disastrous for the credit markets." He turned to Stewart. "Call that Special Agent bitch back and tell her to take the crash and everything in its vicinity out to sea and dump it."

"Sir, the chain of command?" Stewart said.

"Jesus Christ. Call her, then call Franklin. I don't want any delays."

"Yes, sir."

"As for the real reason he crashed . . ." He paused to grab the sides of his head and ride a wave of nausea. "Who the hell knows? Maybe he didn't kill himself. Maybe he was flying over his barn to admire his artwork and goofed. Then again, what kind of idiot tries to ram a biplane through the windpipe of a thunderstorm? The facts are he's gone, and he's got to be replaced quickly by someone Wall Street will bless."

"I don't think we should leave his motives unanswered," Foster said. "Mathews' behavior was a crack in the foundation of how we do things. I know one of the shrinks on the New Freedom Commission of Mental Health who could help. Mathews' urge to paint suggests pent-up pressures that painting alone may not have relieved."

Gage leaned his head back and closed his eyes. "No. For Christ's sake, no! We don't want to have to trust some shrink, especially one of the political bastards on that commission."

"Let's make a different assumption," Hawkins said. "Let's assume he was the same guy we knew. Seems reasonable to me. Any of us any different now than we were a year ago? Not in any radical sense. So if that's true what do we have? His neighbors may have seen him painting the dollar but the desecration of Washington's image was very likely the work of vandals that they didn't see."

"Did vandals paint 'barbarous relic' on his plane, too?" Stewart asked.

"You ask those hangar guys a few more times what they saw, and they'll change their story. Ask them a few more times after that and they'll start peeing and crying. There's no evidence Mathews painted his plane. There will be no witnesses to any alleged evidence."

"That might do it, Hawk," Gage said.

"Those guys won't know what they saw when our Neanderthals finish with them. They should be locked up. We can't run a country while two-bit liars take cheap shots at the government in public."

"We better hope Mathews' camera got destroyed in the crash," Stewart said.

"Huh?" Hawkins said.

"As you might recall, he was a camera freak. He took pictures of table settings if he found them interesting. According to Special Agent Frenzel-Johnson he had one of the hangar workers take a picture of him standing next to the plane before going up. Of course, they could be lying about that too."

"Why didn't you tell us?" Hawkins said.

"I'm telling you now. After the photo shoot he took the camera with him into the cockpit. It's possible he ditched it before he crashed."

"I want every grunt in the goddamn CIA brought to that farm to comb the area for that camera," Gage demanded. "How big is his farm?"

"Forget that," Hawkins snapped. "A biplane can be landed almost anywhere. Someone's back yard. Someone who would take the camera off his hands. But why?"

"The internet," Foster said, "if he had an accomplice."

"He wouldn't need an accomplice if he survived the crash," Stewart said. "It's possible he did since there's no trace of him yet."

"If his plane's in ashes, I doubt he went out trick or treating," Hawkins said.

"If his plane's in ashes, then he should be the same way," Stewart countered.

"Yeah, well, wherever he is, if that picture shows, we'll have ourselves an interesting opportunity," Hawkins said. "We've needed something like this to bring the Net Cops to the fore."

"What the hell's that?" Gage asked.

"The Net Cops -- the PCIPB." Hawkins said, adding impatiently, "Marlowe's group. The President's Critical Infrastructure Protection Board. A group of advisers on computer security issues."

"Don't get that way with me!" Gage snapped. "I can't keep track of all the goddamn commissions we've created, especially with my skull splitting in half."

"Sorry," Hawkins said, momentarily chagrined. "They're developing a thick document called the National Strategy to Secure Cyberspace. It identifies ways to keep riff-raff from disseminating material that exposes . . . sensitive government operations."

"How far along is it?" Gage asked.

"Virtually done."

"Most people wouldn't regard Preston Mathews as riff-raff," Stewart said.

Hawkins looked at him. "What's that supposed to mean?"

"If the picture lands on the internet, Mathews likely had something to do with it. It was his camera. He had the picture taken."

Hawkins was momentarily nonplussed. "There was no camera," he decreed. "That has to be a lie. Mathews had no material motive to go loony. Those guys at the hangar could write the bible for anarchists. They should have their tongues cut out and shoved up their behinds."

"Yeah. And while we're at it, make them parade naked that way down Pennsylvania Avenue," Stewart added. Hawkins gave him a dirty look.

"Christ, you're killing me – both of you," Gage wailed. "It's late and we're way ahead of ourselves. I've got to meet with the thieves at the Fed sometime tomorrow to discuss a temp replacement for Mathews. The goddamn markets will need coddling up the wazoo. The last thing they need to hear is a rumor that the Fed chief laboriously painted a demented picture of the American dollar on the front of his barn then deliberately crashed his biplane at the foot of it."

"Financial market suicides were common during the early days of the Depression," Foster ruminated. "Mathews' death may not be all that shocking."

Gage leaped up and grabbed Foster by the shirt. "Jesus Christ, Foster! What species of idiot—? We're talking about the Fed chairman! Suicide is out of the question! Out of the question! I nominated him for that position, for Christ's sake! And keep your trap shut about 'early days of the Depression'! That was then, this is now, and now there is no depression and never will be. 'Depression' is no longer an economic concept -- *capisce*?!" The blood drained from Foster's face.

Gage doubled over and turned away, falling back on the couch. Stewart grabbed a trash basket and placed it in front of him. Gage spat once in it and braced himself for something bigger. He wheezed words out like a man cradled in death's lap. "Mathews died in a tragic accident. His loss is lamented, but he will be replaced. Monetary policy will continue to hum along just fine." He rolled his head in Stewart's direction. "The apes will keep the farm secured until everything's cleaned up. No one from the press has wormed their way in." He waited for confirmation.

"They're roped out," Stewart said.

"Make sure they stay that way, damn it," Gage said evenly.

Hawkins said, "The president of the United States and the director of the FBI should hold a joint press announcement tomorrow morning. Director Franklin assures the country that Mathews died in a tragic plane crash. Then you assure the country that an interim replacement will be named later that day after meeting with the Fed governors."

"Perfect," Gage said in a flat voice. "Get it arranged."

Stewart's cell phone rang. He took a few steps away from the others as he answered it. "Yeah?"

Moments later he said "Yeah" a second time. He listened, took out a pen, and wrote something on the back of a nearby White House visitor's brochure. Then he mumbled an obscenity and hung up.

"I don't like it when Boy Scouts swear," Gage said.

"That was Terry Parks from the *Times*," Stewart told the others. "An anonymous caller suggested he check out a certain website, then call my number. It's already had over a thousand hits. Hang on."

He went to his laptop with brochure in hand and brought the web page up. "Oh, Jesus!" he said. Suddenly piqued, he slapped the lid shut and tossed the laptop to Hawkins, who caught it with a grunt against his inflated midsection.  He opened the lid.

Hawkins and Gage cursed in unison.  Foster buried his head in his hands and moaned.

There were two photos: A picture of Mathews beaming a huge smile while standing next to the late *Barbarous Relic*, and another of the fully-intact barn with Chief overseeing the world.  The caption under the barn read:

Preston Mathews' masterpiece: The Jolly Roger Dollar.

**6**

The TV announcement at 9 a.m. with FBI director Matt
Franklin went smoothly because Gage dismissed himself
quickly to prepare for a meeting with Federal Reserve officials.
But Hawkins had already met with them, and together they
reached an agreement. Gage would meet with only one
official, Fielding Wallace III, Ph.D. Getting together with all
the governors would eat too much time, Hawkins said, and
fray too many nerves. Huddling with just Wallace would be
politically safe because as vice chairman he outranked the
others.

When Wallace walked into the Oval Office at 10 a.m.
sharp, Gage could tell immediately he would be the right plug
for the gap. A man of average build with a kindly smile and
the sharp eyes of a sniper, Wallace oozed the proper mix of
confidence and deference and showed almost no trace of the
phone call that had started his day eight hours earlier. They
sat at a small table having coffee.

Words flowed between them about the air of disbelief over
Chairman Mathews being gone so suddenly, cut off in the
prime of life, struck down by Mother Nature during a moment
of indiscretion, and how it teaches us to savor each moment as
if it were our last.  Determined to hit a consoling note and
move on, Wallace offered the observation that Mathews, at
least, had no family to leave behind, other than an ex-wife.
"Thank God for small favors," he said, to which Gage grunted
affirmation while suppressing a yawn.

    "The market doesn't like shocks, Mr. President," Wallace
segued, "and this will be a shock.  We can't make it go away,
but we can control its effects."

    "That's our top priority," Gage said.  He thought of his
migraine effects and how they had been controlled last night
by Fann Li, his resident masseuse.  Thanks to a 2:30 a.m.
session with her he could now tolerate light, sounds, and high-
priced sycophants like Wallace.  Everyone knew about Li, even
his globetrotting wife, so he didn't have the burden of keeping
her under covers, so to speak.  Li was originally a loan from
Lamar Gartner, an L.A. TV producer and political activist.
Twice-daily massages kept Gartner's brain from imploding,
and in his relaxed stupor he sometimes promised her the
world, including her own quiet TV show.  Gartner as well as Li
had thought the loan would be for the duration of the
campaign only, but Gage got hooked and decided to keep her
around.  His presidential physician, a Harvard graduate of
oriental descent named Orson Soo Hoo, enthusiastically
approved the demure Li as a necessary tonic for Gage's mental
stability, her services to be taken on an as-needed basis.  Gage,

for his part, considered Li the greatest discovery in the history of medicine.

Wallace handed Gage a single-page document. "This is my proposed communiqué," he said. Gage took the sheet and braced himself with a sip of coffee, reading silently:

> It has been said that when we are born each of us owes God a death. Nevertheless, it is never easy to see this debt collected, especially when the deceased is a good friend and colleague. It is more difficult still when death takes someone in the prime of life.

> Preston Mathews was an exceptional leader with an acute understanding of both domestic and international markets. He was a man committed to the realities of the marketplace, rather than the bias of a theory. In supporting the government's policy of full employment, he made sustainable growth a goal through policies of judicious liquidity. His pragmatic approach to global prosperity earned him plaudits from members of both parties, the financial community, and people all over the world.

> Dr. Mathews would be the first to point out that nineteen people sit at the table in Federal Open Market Committee meetings, twelve of whom have a vote on policy decisions. It is never a one-man rule. Though at times cacophonous, the diversity of viewpoints is a key factor in policymaking.

You don't replace a man of Preston Mathews' stature. But we consider ourselves fortunate that in passing he will serve as a role model as we carry on the Federal Reserve's mission of providing monetary support for the American economy. Our policy goal of seeking maximum sustainable economic growth, therefore, remains unchanged.

Thank you.

Gage nodded and handed the paper back to Wallace. "They'll like it. It says he was a great man and will be missed but you guys can keep the spigots open without him. That's what the investment crowd wants to hear. Wall Street will breathe a sigh of relief."

"Thanks, but I'm a little concerned about Main Street. I wavered on using the word 'liquidity,' but went ahead with it because that's what investors want to hear. It won't mean much to outsiders, though."

"Forget outsiders. That's the reason they're outside – they don't pay attention to terms like 'liquidity.' That's our job. Their job is to keep spending and piling up debt and making their monthly payments. Leave it in."

Wallace chuckled and shifted in his chair nervously. "If only we could use your language instead of mine."

"Yeah, and if we did you know where that'd put us. You never want to stand naked in public. Some kid out there might notice and start a revolution." He laughed, and Wallace found relief in laughing with him.

"The Fed's always been at the mercy of words, Mr. President. We spend more time smithing our announcements than on the decisions that go into them. But it's the way the game is played. It's from our statements that the markets make inferences about the effects of our policies on their plans."

"Inferences," Gage repeated, then laughed. "Inferences! I like it! So much more civilized than 'guesses.'"

Wallace smiled uncertainly.

Gage sobered. "Okay. We'll go on the air together at noon in the press room. We'll get in just before kickoff on the college games, which means a lot of the sets will already be on. I'll make a brief announcement about Mathews then introduce you. When you say 'Thank you,' I'll follow with the same and we'll both walk out. Ignore the questions. Feel free to smile and wave. Leave them thinking there's nothing to worry about."

"Got it."

"And speaking of liquidity," Gage continued, "you and I need to reach an understanding. I'm going to need it more than ever to fund the wars and keep incumbents in office. At the same time we can't have all this liquidity jacking consumer prices up. It's the same-old, same-old, right? You know how hard it is to dress up the price indexes so inflation looks tame. We tell people inflation is mild while their costs are going through the roof. That gets them bitching, but it also gets them thinking. We want them to do as little of that as possible. When we blame price increases on the inherent greed of business or on unavoidable shortages of production, they accept it as self-evident. God help us if they ever think differently. Prices aren't too bad yet because Asians are still hoarding a lot of the dollars they get from the cheap goods they sell us. But can we keep it going?"

"Mr. President, any man who would answer that question with a flat 'yes' shouldn't be trusted. We understand the needs of an active government, and our current solution is showing some fraying at the edges though not much else. But like you say, we depend on foreigners to hold our dollars, or buy American armaments, or lend the national government money. We influence them in many ways, but we can't control them. Someday they may do things differently. They may send those dollars back home."

"But we do control them," Gage countered. "They see our astronomical military budget and cringe—or worse. You might say our dollars are backed with guns instead of gold. We want those little bastards to keep seeing it that way because we have big plans for a lot of tinpot regimes around the world, especially the ones floating on oil, and it's putting a strain on our sources of revenue. I don't want to see a dollar tsunami rolling in from China or Japan. I don't care how you do it, Dr. Wallace, but I want you to keep those dollars off my back. If they land over here . . . well, if they land over here Attila the Hun will be sitting in this chair instead of a nice guy like me." Gage didn't so much as smile, though Wallace croaked a brief chuckle. "I think you get the picture. Your job is to keep the damn dollars overseas."

Wallace nodded solemnly. "I understand, sir. But let's keep the good news in focus. Asian dollar-holders and American consumers are making out pretty darn good. And I must tell you, I'm rather excited about that new TV show Vicki Prentiss is doing about inflation. What's it called? 'The Browns versus the Federal Reserve Note'?"

"'The Browns versus the Dollar.'"

"Much better. It uses the familiar word rather than the more obscure designation."

"We want to keep it obscure, too. A falling dollar is bad enough, but a falling federal reserve note puts light where it's not wanted."

"I see your point."

"I'm not thrilled with the show no matter what it's called. I don't like Americans thinking the dollar is their opposition or enemy. The dollar's supposed to be their ally. They bust their butts for something that's working against them – what does that say about the dollar managers? But I'd rather she use 'dollar' than 'federal reserve note,' for Christ's sake."

"Sir, I understand your reservations, but I think the show will be a good thing," Wallace said. "According to what I've heard it won't attempt to get into monetary details. Essentially, it'll just be regular people sitting around whining about higher prices, only they'll be doing it in front of a TV camera with Vicki moderating their comments. They might actually help one another deal with rising prices. As long as Vicki doesn't experiment with . . . discarded theories, there should be no problem."

"Vicki's not a problem, but who knows what the damn Browns will do? They might get the smart idea they're too visible to fail and try to buy everything in sight. The last thing we need is a six-pack of families going belly-up.  Enough about the Browns.  Are we square here?"

"Yes, sir, I believe we are.  Generally, the country's in good shape, even though the dollar is stooped and losing its hair.  But then, that's the fate of all managed currencies, and the American dollar is still the best out there.  As long as no one here or overseas rocks the boat, by dumping dollars or . . . some other way—"

"—Forget that show, okay?  It won't be a problem."

"I was referring to the stuff on the internet."

"Forget that, too.  No one turns to the internet for real news or opinion.  It's full of riff-raff.  No one trusts it.  It's politically powerless."

"Well, that's . . . good to know," Fielding Wallace attempted to say with conviction.  "I'm confident Asians won't change their policy anytime soon, and Americans will keep gobbling up those great gadgets they make.  And we at the Fed will make sure they'll have the credit to keep buying them."

"Good," Gage said.  He rose from his chair.  Wallace stood up so quickly he almost upended his coffee.  They shook hands.  "And God help the poor bastard who tries to rock the boat," Gage concluded.

7

Nina Stefanelli couldn't believe it.

She was wakened by a phone call at 7:21 a.m. from Red somebody with the FBI who asked if she was the former spouse of Preston Mathews. He put her on hold before she could answer and was treated to the stirring sounds of the *Washington Post March* as performed by the National Symphony Orchestra, a recorded voice said. Seconds later she heard a dial tone: she had been cut off.

In her stupor she was certain her ex was being held prisoner by terrorists and it would be her job to explain to the kidnappers that they had it backwards, that if they wanted to bring the country to its knees set him free and let him do his job as Fed chairman. That was the only reason government tolerated free marketers, she was convinced, so they could argue for the release of one of the state's elites in a hostage situation.

She clicked her TV on to see where it was happening and saw Preston's farm. She saw smoke and what looked like some sort of wreckage with workers and machinery and almost everybody wearing jackets with *FBI* in large luminous letters on the back. Vicki Prentiss from Eagle News was interviewing some guy who was saying Preston Mathews appeared to have been alone when his plane hit the ground, bounced into the front of the barn, and exploded on impact. Nor was there any sign of foul play, such as a bomb. "Looks like just a routine tragedy," the guy said, "but we're not through yet."

She tapped the mute button on her remote and felt her heart pounding horribly. She closed her eyes and waited.

*It doesn't hurt that bad, does it?* she thought. *How could it? How could something this preposterous bring pain? So the Fed chairman crashed and burned . . . You damn fool. What would you expect?*

She felt certain she would cry, but she didn't. That puzzled her.

She reached over to her night stand and dug underneath some papers she had been reading the night before. Her fingers latched onto an encased gold coin dated 1893, long a collector's item and once a token of a husband's love. It had been sitting there unnoticed since . . . since forever, it seemed. But it was time to notice it now. It was time to realize the two would never meet again – Preston and gold. She tossed the coin in the air once and caught it. Then she lobbed it at a trash basket on the other side of the room and missed badly.

*. . . but we're not through yet.* Of course you're not through. But Preston Mathews is.

FBI Red called again and repeated what the TV had told her and apologized for bringing her bad news. Would she be available later to answer some routine questions? Why of course she would and they hung up.

Routine questions. Not probing, routine, the kind that are asked when the answers don't matter or are known in advance. His life wasn't supposed to end like that. His life as Fed enemy, that is, not as Fed chairman. So that's where the great revolution ends, over there on the bedroom carpet between a trash basket and a plastic shopping bag of cotton balls and hand soap she had been intending to put away.

Looking at the coin lying prostate among her junk reminded her of a soldier left dead and forgotten on some battlefield . . . a soldier not killed by his enemies, against whom he was impervious, but through the traitorous acts of his general.

*But that wasn't quite right, was it?* she chided herself. *She* had tossed the coin, *she* had put it to rest. Yes, the coin had been betrayed. And the second time by her.

She joined the fight because she believed in the cause, not Preston or anyone else. She didn't quit when he took the political path to success. Was she quitting now? Would she announce her resignation at the university and seek employment in some government bureaucracy? Would she kill herself too?

Is that what honorable thieves do who seek absolution - go down in a self-inflicted inferno? Suicide would put an end to his guilt, but it wouldn't buy him absolution. For that he would have to take huge measures to undo the damage.

And he would know it.

She was torn up. And confused. And angry. She felt a desire to do something wicked.

She jumped out of bed and retrieved the coin, then headed straight for her bedroom closet.

She owned more garments than would fit comfortably on the clothes racks, but there they hung, nevertheless. Her sweater collection included a joke, a gift from student Greg Reece to mentor Nina. He had brought it back from Australia and told her she could never wear it in public because the cops would be all over her if she did. Legally, she couldn't even wear it in her closet, but in the next few minutes it would be on her back and headed for the boonies.

Without coffee, without brushing teeth or hair -- and without thinking too much about it -- she left Fairfax, followed the interstate west for 18 miles, and now rolled along a two-laner to ex's farm in her Midnight Jeep, fully prepared to walk among the jackboots because she, too, was wearing shades and an FBI raid jacket.

When she got close to the farm she encountered a roadblock -- two vest-wearing mesomorphs and their rolling stock. One of them was engaged in telling a story, judging from his hand gestures. She slowed to a stop. She had a plan, and if it didn't work she would have to fall back on plan B, which she would figure out on the fly. Somewhat irritated, the clean-shaven young storyteller stepped toward her and leaned his face close to her window. She held a hand up to implore his patience then proceeded to dig through her purse, pulling out combs, breath mints, wallet, lipstick, mirror, and other assorted necessities looking for her nonexistent badge.  Quite strategically, she kept her back to the guard with the big letters in front of his eyes while she ransacked her handbag.  He finally had enough and ordered her on through, evidently seduced by the jacket, the grimness of her vehicle, and perhaps her grim lack of a face.  She flashed him a smile, worked the Jeep around their vehicles then gunned forward fifty yards where the now-famous farm was on her left.  She panicked briefly thinking he might have noticed her car tag lacked the proper government imprimatur, but her rear-view mirror confirmed he had gone back to his tale-telling.  She slipped into a spot on the right bank of the road among scattered parked vehicles.

She  got out and quickly pulled her jacket off, then lifted her sunglasses and stared at the farm.  She stood dead still.  A bulldozer was plowing piles of Preston's barn into the back end of a tractor-trailer.  They were demolishing the barn, every bit of it, finishing what the fire had started.  Yellow tape surrounded everything, FBI personnel scurried about like ants over spilled syrup, and far off to the side in front of the house a few media people lounged about the porch.  Two white TV vans and a couple of cars, one of them a lustrous red, sat waiting on the front lawn.

This is real, she thought, hearing the rumble of tractors and men's voices shouting over them.  The TV didn't transmit the scent of a burning barn or the chill of the wind on her face. The TV version seemed more like a Hollywood production that could be rearranged at the director's will.  *Let's shoot that scene over, this time with the plane crashing over here.*

Nina was physically fit for an economics prof and had the chiseled-cheekbone, dark-eyed look of a mid-40s Mrs. Peel from *The Avengers* TV series of long ago, but unlike the fictional character her acts of daring were pretty much limited to late-night trips to Waffle House. She had anger working for her now, though, and it would do nicely for her lack of courage.

She crossed the road and headed up the gravel driveway, looking for a certain woman and her cameraman. She found her talking to a guy smoking a cigarette behind one of the vans.

"Excuse me," Nina said, removing her sunglasses. "I'm Nina Stefanelli, the crash victim's ex." To Vicki, she said: "Perhaps you remember me."

"Terry Parks," said the guy. Parks hovered somewhere near 40, with a slim build and intense eyes.

"Hello," Nina said.

"Hi, Nina," Vicki said in greeting an old acquaintance.

Vicki Prentiss had the kind of looks and poise that ten years earlier would have swept all honors at any beauty pageant. Even today her effect on people was hypnotic, and her evening TV journal was critical to Eagle's 6.6 rating in the 18-49 demographic. In reviewing the first installment of her new show, "The Browns versus the Dollar," one commentator said it had the potential to be the perfect vehicle to correct her one perceived flaw, that of being too remote. As a biannual event, however, the program would not air often enough to do the job. "You almost want to see the market dip to get her show on more often."

"You have something for us?" Vicki asked Nina.

"Not about the crash. But I would like to make a few comments on the Preston Mathews I once knew. On air."

"It's been awhile since our last talk."

"A few years."

"You seemed to be stuck in the past."

"Not stuck at all. I'm there quite willfully, on certain issues."

"What would you like to talk about?" Parks asked her.

Nina pulled the encased gold coin from her purse and held it out. "This. He gave it to me as a wedding present. I kept it after the divorce. People should know that the printer they admired so much was once a staunch advocate of honest money."

"Printer!" Parks burst out, chuckling.

Vicki didn't smile. "There will be bios written that will cover that phase of his life. We don't need to go into that now. It has nothing to do with his death."

"I think it might," Nina said, "even if it turns out to be an accident. And it looks like the FBI has confirmed that it--"

"They've confirmed zilch so far," Parks said,. "Until they recover a body or remains we don't know who died, if anyone."

"I'd say they had a pretty good idea," Vicki said.

"But we don't know, damn it! We're talking about the Lord of Interest Rates. And we don't know for sure if he's dead or not."

"The government doesn't want to turn this thing into a gruesome freak show. Yes, he was the Fed chairman. And if he doesn't pass away smoothly we could have a market meltdown on our hands."

"Sure." Parks fumed. "No question. We need to protect our house of cards from any pin drop. Besides, why waste taxpayer money digging for the truth when we already know what it is?" He turned to Nina and pointed to the FBI activity. "They're not digging. They're burying. They don't want any embarrassing facts popping up to deflate the Dow."

"I'm biased, I admit," Vicki said. "I've always had a preference for prosperity over depression. Why don't you show her that website, while you're at it?"

Parks smiled and looked at Nina.

He led them to a candy apple red 1969 Mustang Cobra 428 in mint condition. "My baby. Don't touch, please," he said with a wink. He retrieved a laptop from the front passenger seat, popped the lid, worked his fingers over the keys and scroll pad, then turned the screen to Nina.

"I showed these to the folks at the demolition party over there, but they turned their noses up. I predict they'll be as famous as the one of Rumsfeld gladhanding Hussein in December of '83." Vicki rolled her eyes.

The photos on the screen faded rapidly in and out of Nina's consciousness, as if her brain kept rejecting the images sent from her eyes. But it wasn't the images, she realized – not exactly. Those were there in front of her: the picture of Preston with the Barbarous Relic biplane, the one of his barn with the skull-and-crossbones dollar. What bothered her was what the images were doing. They were exhuming her hope, for God's sake, and she couldn't deal with that. She slipped into her professorial shell and tightened her grip on the gold piece. "Where did these come from?" she managed.

"Ah! That's the question. No one's 'fessed up."

"And whoever did it was probably trick or treating last night," Vicki said.

"You, Sweetheart, are in a state of denial. But I forgive you." He turned to Nina. "See the little owl up there on the loft?" he said, pointing at the laptop's screen. "Vicki noticed him, not me."

"What about it?" Nina asked.

"We've seen it flying around here this morning," Vicki said as if conceding a point.

"Looks like he lived there," Parks added. "And now he's got no home. It doesn't prove anything, but it suggests the barn in this picture was really Mathews'. Not only that, it suggests the picture was taken recently -- judging from the sunlight I'd say yesterday afternoon -- because the owl is hanging around now like an evicted tenant with no place to go. And how many trick or treaters have photo access to Mathews' barn?"

Nina frowned. "Then there's the FBI's sealed lips . . ."

"Right," Parks said. "But there's something else. You listening, Vicki? They're saying the plane bounced into the barn and exploded. The mortifying mural, therefore, was obliterated, if it ever existed. I was here shortly after they arrived last night. The plane was a burning hulk -- in front of the barn. The barn wasn't hit. That's no small lie they're trying to hide. The plane didn't destroy the painting, it spotlighted it. Did the pilot light his plane there for that purpose? We'll never know. You should've seen what it looked like -- the pirate dollar, illuminated by the vengeful flames of the *Barbarous Relic*. On All Hallows' Eve, no less. But they made quick work of it and put their tape up to keep us at a distance. Too dangerous, you see."

"If I were them I wouldn't want us around there, either," Vicki said. "Not everything they do is a cover-up. If they had let us roam around at will and the barn blew up, this place would be swarming with lawyers. But that won't stop conspiracy nuts from rallying around these pictures." She sighed. "It would be fun to put you both in front of a camera to talk about this stuff, but Eagle News won't touch it. Don't fret -- *Potomac Plowshare* will eat it up. This is their meat and potatoes."

"Quite possibly *Plowshare* created barbarous-relic.com," Parks said.

"You mean it's possible they didn't?" Vicki said.

Nina's heart leaped. "Is that the name of this website?"

"Yup," Parks said, nodding at the laptop. "Great name, huh?"

## 8

The Gage administration cranked up the damage-control machine.

It sent expert mouths to the Sunday morning talk shows to assure viewers that contrary to rumors, the Preston Mathews story was nothing more than a tragic accident.

"The sensationalism surrounding his death is the work of vandals and liars, quite frankly," Hawkins told his interviewer, a quiet middle-aged man with round shoulders and an ingratiating smile. "You have to remember that any time a prominent member of government dies suddenly the air is rife with innuendo, speculation, and outright falsehoods. And because of the proliferation of low-cost digital devices and point-and-click software, many of the people with a grudge against government find it easy to manufacture grossly misleading media and transmit it over the internet."

"Do you think this tragedy will bring a call for reform? Regarding the internet?" the interviewer asked.

"No question. Most Americans won't tolerate this kind of abuse. The Gage Administration will be working closely with their congressional representatives, and together we will put a stop to the hateful slander of a few misfits that can ruin a good man's reputation and possibly disrupt the smooth-running of society."

"Some people will say your proposal is an infringement on freedom. How would you respond?"

"They're got it exactly backwards. We're culling abuse from the system, not freedom. A restriction on slander is not a restriction on freedom, as any legal scholar will testify. It will be a safety and security measure, and will, therefore, protect the freedom we have."

On Monday morning Fielding Wallace III stood before a packed house in the New York Waldorf's grand ballroom and assured jittery financiers that the Federal Reserve was bigger than any one man. He cited examples of large corporations that were hit with the sudden loss of CEO's, CFO's, presidents, ace programmers, and other prominent personnel. "As unwelcome as these situations were, the companies are structured so that they don't miss a beat. Their market shares don't suffer. They continue to innovate and produce products that people buy. That, in fact, is the mark of a great leader. He or she raises the level of the people around them. And in so doing the show doesn't close when they leave."

The Fed, he told them, "was in the unique position of being in the public spotlight, which is where it should be. For this reason there will always be a handful of individuals who will attempt to monkey-wrench the system. We're all familiar with hackers who write computer viruses just to spread havoc around the world. So it is with large public agencies like the Fed whose leaders become the target of hateful or irresponsible rumors. Some of us have heard stories that are quite imaginative. Well, I'll admit, they might interest Hollywood, but they're of no interest to us.

"All of you knew Preston Mathews as a responsible individual and the best friend the markets ever had. Let me give you some advice: Remember him that way and go back to work. That's what we at the Fed are doing."

The crowd at the Waldorf gave him a standing ovation.

Monday afternoon the stock market closed in a slight decline. By Tuesday's closing it was past the point of Fateful Friday's closing averages. All was well in investor land.

At least for a day. By close of business Wednesday the Dow had dropped 141 points. Hawkins knew why, and he knew who could fix things.

Treasury Secretary Benjamin Levy didn't like his job. He didn't mind so much heading up the collection of tributes to the government because it was a dirty job and someone had to do it. Government, he believed, was a necessary evil that could only be funded by some form of systematic theft, such as overt taxation. But God, how he loathed the politics! He had people buried twenty levels deep in their org chart doing "mission-critical" work, whose names and jobs he had never heard of, earning a king's ransom and occupying a plush office where they monitored their real businesses. Shouldn't the top dog at least know who's working for him and what they do? At budget reviews he was expected to sign off on new slots without question, because some other power holder owed someone else a favor.

Yet he had to concede it was to his short-run advantage. Everyone everywhere considered growth a sign of health, and since "overweight" had no meaning in government, every organization was forever larding its loins as a way of achieving political invincibility. With a logic unique to government, the bigger one of its entities became the more immunity it had to efficiency experts, who saw only the leanest of meat in the overstuffed organizations and nothing but waste and fat in the politically weaker ones. Levy thus had countless deputy assistant secretaries under him busying themselves with the nebulous and irrelevant, coordinating this and analyzing that, fighting box cutters in the banks, in the credit unions, in the foreign exchanges, in any and every way that money bears on human life, which is to say everything from Girl Scout cookies to the biggest multinationals.

It all but obscured the one role that counted: keeping the citizens sufficiently indoctrinated to pay up – willingly.

Gage had picked Levy on Hawkins' recommendation, and Hawkins liked Levy for his military background, his name, and the fact that he was physically fit and slim. Levy, at 54, was in fact a fitness center spectacle. At five-foot eight and 155 pounds, he could pump out 100 repetitions of a 100-pound bench press at the Treasury's gym, shower, then swim a mile in the Olympic pool alternating between the Australian crawl and the racing backstroke.

On the day after the latest Dow Drop, Levy met with three senior officials from the Bureau of Engraving and Printing and decided afterward he was in desperate need to shoot something. The meeting had not gone well. His subordinates had presented spineless non sequiturs about how Mathews acquired $100,000 in hundred dollar bills for his Trick or Treat flight over Morrisville.

Their spokesperson was a short middle aged man named Riley who spoke so quietly Levy had to strain to hear him. He was perfect for the job because he always spoke that way, and Levy could never accuse him of being suppliant, though that's how he came across. He remembered being in a room reading a report once while Riley and a clerk were in an adjacent office with the door open. It was comical. He could hear the clerk fine and Riley not at all. The clerk would ask a question then moments later ask a follow-up question with no intervening answer, at least not one Levy could detect. It was as if the clerk were talking to himself.

Along with the others, Riley had at hand a bottle of water, a perennial element of every meeting Levy held. Riley clung to his for support. "At this point in our investigation," he said in his barely audible style, "it appears he took the money without our knowledge and without proper authorization." He cleared his throat.

Levy couldn't help smile. "So, Preston Mathews robbed the B.E.P.?"

Riley glanced for support at his two colleagues, cleared his throat again, and turned back to Levy. "We don't have enough information to rest comfortably with that conclusion. We can neither affirm nor—"

"—Are we in the habit of leaving money lying around?"

"Ah, no, sir, we're not. . . Our security procedures are unsurpassed. This is the first blemish on our record."

"The first what?"

"Blemish."

"But you're reasonably sure the money left when he did."

"As far as we can tell, yes." Levy felt an urge to throw something at him, to see if he would at least raise his voice in protest.

"So tell me: How does one man EVER walk out of the B.E.P. with a hundred thousand dollars?"

Riley cleared his throat and took a sip of water. His voice rose a bit in volume. "One man doesn't, sir, unless he's the Fed chairman."

"The Fed chairman . . . ?"

"He's next to God."

Hawkins called and invited himself along before Levy could escape. As far as their secretaries and the rest of the world were concerned, Hawkins and Levy were taking a little afternoon R & R at Levy's West Virginia ranch near White Sulphur Springs, hunting wild turkey. But Levy had no interest in shooting birds. He had his maintenance workers nail together some boards and prop them up to resemble the side of a barn. At Levy's direction, one of them slapped some paint on the wood to approximate a U.S. dollar with a Jolly Roger in the center. They then hauled it to the bottom of a small rise near the edge of some woods, and Levy proceeded to blast it to bits with his Winchester 12-gauge shotgun.

Hawkins declined to join him and stood back watching while drawing slowly on a Cuban Robusto, amused at the way the gun kicked the rawboned shooter with each trigger squeeze. When the shooting ended they retired to Levy's den around a pool table, where Levy accepted Hawkins' offer of a Robusto and poured them some JD No. 7 on the rocks.

Levy dragged pensively on his cigar and blew the smoke out. "So, you want me to attack Morrisville, Virginia," he said.

"Just show up with some guns. A little gathering for the evening news."

"What's wrong with garnishing their taxes?"

"Nothing, of course. But we also need a little show."

"Flex some muscle."

"You got it."

Levy flicked his cigar at an ashtray. "You're feeding the enemy."

"No, we're restoring public confidence."

"The public wasn't confident, they were intimidated. They're still that way. Showing up with troops when none are needed will convey weakness. You have nothing to gain by squashing Morrisville."

"General, there's a fire burning. We need to squelch it."

"It's a campfire. It'll burn itself out."

Hawkins moved closer to Levy. "Mathews had a plan. We don't know exactly what it was, but we're pretty sure it's not finished. He apparently has confederates, and his dramatic exit has won him more than a few sympathizers. A quiet announcement about garnishing Morrisville's taxes will soothe the public's resentment, but they need reminding about who's in charge. They need to see power. *The markets have to see power.* They have to know we damn well mean business."

"Is Gage behind it?"

"One hundred percent. Along with every bank and investment house on Wall Street."

Levy sighed. "I've put on shows before. I could always make a speech, bring along a goon squad."

"They need to feel the heel, Ben. All people do, whether they're a free people like ours or the other kind."

"Feel the heel." Levy smirked.

"What's so funny?"

"Oh, nothing. Just thinking about my purpose in life. The older you get, the more you like to think you had one. I became a military man to defend freedom. Now I'm the damn Treasury secretary . . ."

"So what's the problem? You're defending your country in a different way."

"I was wondering what I'm defending it against."

"Has the JD affected your brain? You just spent a half-hour blowing his damn dollar to bits."

"I needed to hit something. I'm not sure I picked the right target."

"Ben, listen: You're defending the country against crucifixion on a cross of gold. The yellow metal almost put us out of business in the 1930s. We don't want to repeat a mistake of that magnitude. There is not a single reputable economist who supports a gold standard. It's dangerous, it's a threat to prosperity. It will reduce a modern economy to ashes -- that's the real symbolism in Mathews' crack up. You've got to stand up for the way things work now. And that takes a show of muscle."

Levy flicked an ash that wasn't there and shook his head slowly, confused.

"Look, Ben, the people need to see us as more than paper shufflers and lawmakers. We can't defend civilization with words alone. We need guns. We need rugged men willing and able to use those guns. And the people need to see these guys. If we don't have the guts to get tough we might as well turn the country over to the fascists."

"You don't feel at all hypocritical?"

"Hell, no. Why should I?"

"Jesus, Tom. Mathews did for Morrisville what he's been doing for the whole of government and the big banks. That doesn't bother you?"

"No, for Christ's sake! The government's held to different standards. Everyone knows it and accepts it. Government is force. Our methods, therefore, are expedient. We give up lucrative careers in the private sector to keep this country together, by any means possible. I'm not bothered by anything we have to do or say. Don't get Jeffersonian on me."

"I wasn't."

"You were about to. Talk about hypocrites, the author of the Declaration of Independence was a goddamn slaveholder. But we took our cue from Honest Abe. With the smart use of force we're setting the world free. A few people get roughed up along the way, maybe, but what the hell. That's a lesson all the great presidents learned, and all the others didn't."

"Government is force. How stupid of me to forget."

"Well, we don't post it on billboards. People like to think they're acting on their own volition." Hawkins sighed. "So, General, can we count on your help?"

"Sure, hell. I'm a soldier. I do what my superiors tell me, whether I like it or not."

**9**

County police officer Brian Mashburn raised his hands above the clamor and waited. The standing-room only crowd in Kamura's Tae Kwon Do studio didn't make him wait long. At six-two and 29 years old, Mashburn was not known to suffer fools gladly or any other way. As he lowered his arms the only chatter remaining came from a young mother shushing her twin toddler sons in the back of the room.

Mashburn looked from face to face and smiled. "Nothing like pocketbook issues to get a full house, is there? I want to welcome everyone, including those of you I haven't seen before. I ask only that y'all give Suzanne your complete attention and save your concerns for the Q&A after." He turned to a mid-thirties woman on his right. "They're all yours, Madam Mayor."

"Thanks, Brian." Suzanne Ward, carrying a white business envelope, moved to the center in front, swapping places with Mashburn.

An attractive woman with short dark hair, Suzanne once had locks that flowed almost to her waist during her anti-imperialism days at the University of Virginia. She still bore a *Don't Tread on Me* tattoo on her upper right arm, an inspiration from her major, American History. She had two kids from a marriage to a doctor then worked as a software tester at Baltimore Gas & Electric. With a low tolerance for corporate life she secured freelance contracts from firms in Richmond, D.C., and Baltimore before moving to Morrisville, which roughly centered her between the three cities.

As she looked over the packed house at Kamura's that evening, she wondered if any of them, including her, had the stomach for a rebellion. If they had been around in 1773 would they have helped dump the King's tea in Boston Harbor as a protest against a government-chartered monopoly? Had American public education killed the rebel spirit in its citizens? In 1787 Jefferson wrote to a man named Smith that we wouldn't make it as a country if the people didn't overthrow their government every 20 years or so. Lethargy, he noted, was death to the public liberty.

Was she about to address an assembly of political zombies?

"As most of you know," she began, "I've spent the last couple of days on the phone. Although the conversations have left me drained, the real shocker came in the mail today, as you'll see." She waved the envelope some. "But first, let me attempt to summarize our situation.

"Treasury is calling our good fortune a windfall. More importantly, they're calling it *their* windfall. They're saying the missing money is the town's liability -- a debt we owe them.

Therefore, they've decided to garnish our property taxes until they recover the amount they lost, one hundred thousand dollars. They magnanimously waived their option to add a fine to the garnishment. When I asked their rep, Mr. Zuccarelli, how they could fine us for picking up money dropped from a biplane, I was told any time a person acquires a possession of the U.S. government without its permission, he's subject to a penalty. According to him, our ignorance about the source of the money is no excuse. Personally, I had to keep reminding myself we're dealing with the government and not the Mafia.

"Some of you didn't collect a cent, others did pretty good. It makes no difference to Treasury. We're all equally guilty and will bear the same penalty."

"I think the whole thing stinks!" a man called out. Others kicked in their agreement.

"How long will they be pickin' our pocket?" another man asked.

"I don't know. They haven't set a payment schedule yet. If that's what we end up doing, I'm going to push for the longest one we can get because with inflation we're better off paying them back in cheaper dollars. Are they legally in the right? Hugh Trombley, our attorney, tells me we're in a legal no-man's land. He also reminds me that they make the rules, and those rules tend to favor the government, strangely enough. Since the Treasury pays the salaries of our court system employees, including the judges, there's little reason to believe they'd rule in our favor."

"Wait a minute!" said Lee Hines, a beefy young garage-gas station owner with a thick black beard. "Our taxes pay the Treasury's salary. They can't thumb their noses at us."

"Yeah, they can, Lee. Unless we're a privileged group, we either pay taxes or go to jail. The Treasury gets our money whether we like what they're doing or not."

"That's not the way it's supposed to work," Hines countered.

"I know. But in any case, the rest of the country is not going to rise up in protest even if they sympathized with us, which, to put it mildly, they don't."

"We're screwed," Hines said.

"That's what I thought," Suzanne said, "until the mail came today."

She opened the envelope, pulled out a two-page letter, and raised it above her head. The first page was printed on embossed letterhead stationery. "No government likes bad publicity. We may not stand a chance legally, but this might be the way to get them to ameliorate or possibly withdraw the garnishment. Now, take that as my heart speaking, not my head. The few people I've shared this with said it's a complete hoax, a prank, and if I had any sense I'd just toss it. Maybe I'm blind but I don't agree - not yet, at least. Let me read it to you and see what you think.

"Dear Mayor Ward," she began.

"As we all know, it has been the policy of government to spend money in record amounts, year after year. Ultimately, the money they spend is ours, but they can't collect it all in taxes without risking their jobs or perhaps their heads. So they've devised less obvious methods of wringing money out of us.

"You saw a crude example of one such method during the Halloween thunderstorm.

"On that day a biplane flew over Morrisville and showered it with freshly printed federal reserve notes. The money arrived, as it were, out of thin air.

"Please note: This money was not taxed away from other citizens and given to you. The money that fell from the plane had no previous owner. It was printed on a printing press. It was created, so to speak, out of thin air.

"What do we call a person who prints money on a printing press? Ask your kids.

"We've read that the pilot of that biplane was the Chairman of the Federal Reserve Board, Preston Mathews, who died a short while later when his plane crashed. The chairman of the Fed has various responsibilities, the most important of which by far is to keep government awash in money. But how is this possible, unless the Fed also collects taxes?

"In its own devious way, it does. It collects taxes by depreciating the currency. Every time it prints more money it steals value from the dollar, so that over time it buys less. Printing money and giving it to the government to spend inflates the money supply. That is what inflation is -- the increase in the total amount of money. The Fed poses as our foremost inflation fighter. The truth is the exact opposite. It is the sole engine of inflation in society.

"It takes time for prices to rise, which gives initial users of the new money the advantage of buying things at current prices. That's nice for the big shots, but by the time the money circulates into less gilded hands the upward pressure on prices has begun.

"As it turns out the first users of the new money are either some agency of government or one of its favored supporters. But that's only the beginning. Since the new money is deposited in a bank, the banking system cleans up, too. Through duplicitous lending practices, commercial banks can multiply the Fed's initial increase by nine-fold, severely magnifying the inflationary effect. The people who benefit from this racket would prefer the rest of you not know about it.

"But now you do, and I have a suggestion. Morrisville is in the news. Take advantage of it. Call a press conference. Read this letter aloud. And to Mr. Benjamin Levy, the Treasury Secretary, I say this: On Halloween eve, the Fed chairman chose to increase the money supply by a microscopic amount to make public a few facts about government-controlled money.

"Therefore, under our current system of money management, which is a major hoax, the money pocketed by the people of Morrisville is as much theirs as the money pocketed by the government. Do you really believe, Mr. Levy, it's in the government's interest to come down hard on Morrisville over the hundred grand I distributed?"

The room inhaled in unison.

Suzanne turned to the second page and continued reading.

"Yes, you read that last sentence correctly.

"Very truly yours,

"Preston Vincent Mathews

"Chairman of the Board of Governors

"United States Federal Reserve"

The outbursts collided with one another: "Jesus Christ!" "I don't believe it!"

"When was it postmarked?" Lee Hines cried out.

Suzanne Ward smiled. "Yesterday."

After the meeting she dug out the name and number of Mathews' ex-wife on the internet and gave her a call. Nina listened without interrupting then insisted on driving to Morrisville right away. Suzanne gave in, admitting it would save her from taking her kids out late at night.

Nina brought a couple of birthday cards along Preston had given her years ago, to make a crude comparison of signatures. For Nina they were unnecessary. As soon as she saw the letter she knew it was legitimate. She handed the cards to Suzanne and looked away, her mind running over thoughts that made no sense.

## 10

A convoy of twenty-three black limousines and a school bus pulled into Morrisville the following day at 2:25 p.m.  By three o'clock Levy and locals were listening to a band of high school kids play *Stars and Stripes Forever* on a podium set up in the town square.  While leading the applause afterward, Levy moved behind a lectern his men rolled out and thanked the kids as they marched back to their bus playing *Yankee Doodle*. Stolid-looking men in suits and sunglasses flanked him and circulated through the crowd, protecting the Secretary from his terrorist enemies in Morrisville, Virginia.  Suzanne Ward and her kids stood in front of the gathering among the photographers and journalists capturing Levy's performance.

He was no longer the same man who sipped JD in his pool room and viewed the world with a healthy cynicism.  He was now an actor putting on a show.

"You know, folks," he began in a serious voice, "terrorists will stop at nothing to bring down our society.  In Salt Lake City just the other day terrorists captured a plane-load of politicians . . . and threatened to release them one by one until their demands were met." He paused for a few polite laughs. "Needless to say, their demands were met on the spot."

As the tittering faded he glanced down at Suzanne, as if his next words were meant for her personally. "Without question, it takes money to bring the torch of liberty to the world's suffering masses and to carry on our never-ending programs here at home." He raised his glance and swept it over the rest of the crowd, his political self shifting into high. "The richest and most generous people in the history of the planet have undertaken a huge responsibility, and we cannot pursue our quest in any but the most responsible way.

"There is scarcely a government in the world that does not get foreign aid from us. And that aid doesn't include the military bases we have in 135 of the world's 192 countries so that people almost everywhere can enjoy the blessings of peace. Domestic spending covers our needs from the crib through retirement, and includes education, health care, housing, defense, homeland security, and numerous independent establishments and government corporations such as the CIA, NASA, AMTRAK, and the Office of Government Ethics. The list of ways government helps us is virtually endless, as is the revenue required to fund those services.

"That is why I want to personally commend you people here, the proud residents of Morrisville, Virginia, for your understanding regarding the windfall you came upon recently. The residents of Morrisville understand this money is not theirs, nor was it duly authorized to be distributed to them.

They understand it is held in trust by the department I have been asked to oversee, the United States Treasury. They understand that, as small as the amount may be relative to national expenditures, they need to put aside any parochial concerns and do what is right for their country. They realize that money taken from the government trust is money taken from some child's education, or it represents food taken from the mouths of families not as fortunate as they are. Because of your understanding and eagerness to cooperate fully, my department has struck an agreement with your mayor, the Honorable Suzanne Ward. Beginning in three months, Morrisville will set aside a number of small payments from their property tax account for the restitution of the funds lost from the Treasury.

"Mayor Ward," Levy said, reaching to one of his agents, who handed him a large wooden plaque, "you and your fellow townspeople have shown such outstanding cooperation in handling this unprecedented windfall, that the United States Department of the Treasury has decided to award the town of Morrisville, Virginia this plaque, to commemorate your dedication to the national interest." He extended his hand to Suzanne and smiled. "Mayor Ward?"

*He knows,* Suzanne thought -- *he knows about the letter and this is his way of burying it.*

The applause around her goaded her into action. She stepped up to the podium numb from the tenderizing and accepted Levy's gift. Levy did the Politician's Pause, freezing his body and smile at the moment she took the plaque and shook his hand. The cameras below them clicked and purred. It was Morrisville's finest hour, and the crowd ate it up. He released her and with an open hand invited her to take the lectern and speak.

The applause subsided. The Treasury Secretary had taken a step to her left and stayed there, apparently not wanting to give her any sense of independence. His bevy of stern bodyguards stood planted around her like executioners waiting in the wings. Below, she could see media people capturing her every hesitating breath and indecisive gesture. The quiet was unnerving. She needed time to think. She had none.

She had carried Mathews' letter to the lectern with her. She had practiced reading it so her delivery would be persuasive. Seeing the *Don't Tread on Me* tattoo in the bathroom mirror that morning had boosted her confidence. Seeing her townspeople now breathless with anticipation curdled her stomach.

She believed in Mathews' words, and that made her Ben Levy's enemy. But he was offering her a devil's deal. If she went along with his charade good things might happen. A run for the Senate, possibly -- her popularity might be high enough. Her parents might even speak to her again.

"Secretary Levy," she began, then stopped.

*Christ, was this how Preston Mathews felt when the ladder to power stared him in the face, needing only to affirm the requisite mantra?* She was nothing, politically, but this accident of history could change that. All she had to do was polish a few boots.

"--this is a totally unexpected surprise," she continued.

And who could blame her for capitulating? People whored themselves all the time for short-sighted advantages. It was the very definition of human existence. Did she really give a damn if the world went to hell? No – a thousand times, no! Why should she take a stand for the good and the right? It pays nothing. Her hero days ended when she took the job with Baltimore G & E. All she wanted now was financial security and good health for her family. This was no time to get principled.

"--and I wish to thank you for taking time from your busy schedule to make this personal visit."

That's it! You're playing along! Forget Suzanne Ward, the woman struggling with self-respect. You're someone special now, because they're making you special. This is how it's done. You don't get it by being a bump in the road. You get it by--

"--Cooperation. That's an idea we don't see honored too often."

You're doing great. Just keep that damn letter out of sight and you'll finish that way. Your neighbors out there all have their hearts in their throats. They desperately want you to play along but are terrified you won't. You're their mayor, for God's sake. You represent them. They don't want any trouble. *They - don't - want - any - trouble.*

"--It is worthy of honor when two or more people join in pursuit of a goal that improves our well-being."

And well-being means your kids. Look at them -- staring at you with liquid eyes. David, fascinated with wildlife since moving to the country, talks about being a biologist someday. Beautiful Denise was smiling with such pride she might burst.

Your kids -- you'd steal for them, you know it, nothing else matters but them. Stop with this stupid hesitation. Just go on with the damn show.

"--If you had awarded this plaque in the name of 'complicity,' however, there would be some trace of honesty in your presentation. While there is no disputing the money showered on our little town did not belong to us, there are underlying issues here crying out for the light of day. I have a letter I'd like to read to you that will explain what I mean . . ."

## 11

The fallout from Suzanne Ward's Last Stand was nonexistent in the Establishment media.  The providers of televised evening news ran the same nineteen seconds of edited video showing the band, Levy, and Suzanne all happily appearing, in succession, on the Morrisville town square, with a reporter doing a voice-over to the effect that reasonable minds had agreed the U.S. Treasury will garnish the locals' property taxes until their debt was repaid.  As one anchor wrapped it up, "An unidentified thief had scattered the money over this little town thirty-eight miles west of Washington during a Halloween Eve thunderstorm, and until today's announcement the problem lingered as to how best to return the amount lost, believed to be roughly one hundred thousand dollars, to the U.S. Treasury.  In other news, . . ."

Americans who rely on TV news to stay informed of important events were not shown Levy nudging Mayor Ward aside as she started to read the letter, knocking the plaque off the lectern and sending the cherished chunk of wood tumbling to the ground. They didn't see him say to the crowd, "You need a new mayor, Morrisville," then walk off stiff-backed with his bodyguards. Nor did they hear Suzanne's response, her voice quavering slightly: "I agree with you, Mr. Secretary. I have no business being in politics. In fact, I'll be making an announcement as soon as I'm done reading this. You might want to stick around."

And of course Levy didn't, nor did TV viewers see Suzanne Ward read the letter and identify its authorship.

When she finished the only announcement she thought about making was a question regarding the whereabouts of her kids. It was an awkward moment, with part of the crowd walking off and the rest chatting among themselves and dispersing slowly, ignoring the embarrassment on the podium. Their mayor had been unspeakably rude, and they were seeking to prop one another up while groping for answers. "Ben Levy was a hell of a nice guy. She could've shown him that letter in private," a man said. No one cheered or applauded or even looked in her direction. Even Lee Hines was silenced. People pretty much acted like the podium was vacant . . . even while she stood on it afterward calling out her kids' names. She finally stepped down to do some legwork, leaving Levy's plaque lying ignominiously on the turf. She found them sulking in the back seat of her car.

"I'm sorry if I disappointed you," she said during the long drive back home, which was the usual 12-minute trip. They said nothing. When she reached the garage at the house they hustled out of the car before she got it into park. She clicked the engine off and leaned her face against the steering wheel, her chest heaving in quiet sobs.

That evening the town fathers met at Kamura's and unanimously appointed Officer Brian Mashburn their interim mayor. They also agreed on a letter of apology for their ex-mayor's mortifying behavior. The gutless entreaty began thusly:

> We, the undersigned and duly-elected spokespersons for the town of Morrisville, Virginia, wish to express our profound appreciation for your department's generous award in recognizing our cooperation in settling a recent pecuniary matter.

They wanted to include a picture of all them smiling and gathered around the plaque, but it had disappeared. Figuring some kid took it as a prank they agreed to post a $100 reward for its safe return. No one bothered to call Suzanne and tell her she was no longer mayor.

She got the news later when David burst into her bedroom shortly after midnight, telling her she had to come quick and see something on his computer. Heartened that her son was speaking to her again, she threw on a robe and followed him.

"It can't be him," Maxwell Gage said, looking at the image on the monitor. "That's ridiculous." The picture showed an attractive young woman proudly holding the plaque Levy had presented to Ward. About ten feet behind her, standing in the shadows, was a man who bore a striking likeness to the late Fed chairman. The caption underneath read, "Barbie Relic captures lost plaque after mayor stands tall in Morrisville. Details below." It was an indoors shot. On a wall behind them was a poster of the Jolly Roger Dollar.

Gage turned and looked up at Mel Stewart, who glanced without success for moral support at Thomas Hawkins standing on the other side of their boss. Stewart had received a tip earlier about a new entry on barbarous-relic.com and checked it out. He brought Hawkins into the know, who in turn summoned Gage from a session with Fann Li. His mood soured by the interruption, Gage threw a robe over his pajama bottoms but didn't bother putting anything on his feet.

"Sir," Stewart began, "the agency never recovered any remains. It's always been an assumption."

"I would guess it's a pretty good assumption, wouldn't you, Stewart? Not too many people would survive a plane crash that explodes into a fireball. Why else would he be positioned so far behind her in this photo? He's an impostor, plain and simple. He and this . . . *female* are pranksters having fun at our expense. Get the FBI on it and find out who they are."

Gage started to get up. "There's more to it," Stewart said.

"The picture links to a video," Hawkins said.

"It covers the whole circus," Stewart said. "Someone in Morrisville took video and posted it on this site."

Gage sat down and clicked on the picture. A video played that began with the Sousa march and ended with Suzanne Ward looking around in confusion for her kids. The final frame frozen on the screen showed Suzanne brushing a strand of hair back from her face. Gage sat in the chair staring at the display, taking deep breaths.

"We don't believe the mayor had any connection to the video," Stewart continued, "not at this point. She doesn't once look at the camera during her talk."

"The video can be downloaded," Hawkins added. "We expect it will spread far and wide."

"Jesus Christ," Gage muttered, now focusing on a bland portion of the wall in front of him. "These goddamn migraines have a will of their own." Stewart pulled a vial from his pants pocket. Gage saw him peripherally and shot an arm out to stop him. "No! No pills." He closed his eyes and kept them closed. "Call Marlowe now, and tell the bastard I want his butt here at 10 a.m. Get Levy over here, too, and our new money printer. If I've got anything else scheduled—"

"—You're scheduled to read nature books to a class in Buffalo, Missouri at eleven," Stewart said. "It's part of your 'Knowledge is Freedom' campaign."

Gage's eyes opened, sickly and stressed. "—If I've got anything else scheduled clear it. Marlowe is going to tell us how to fix this problem permanently. In the meantime shut down this goddamn website."

"How do we get around the First Amendment?" Stewart asked.

Gage lifted his head and gazed at Stewart in startled disbelief. The big dope was serious.

"We'll get it done, Chief," Hawkins said.

## 12

With one exception the assembled personages in the White House meeting room the following morning presented themselves with the usual shine, helped considerably by massive quantities of a popular psychoactive drug served in fine Lenox china cups. Accompanying the leaded beverages was a sumptuous spread of Racine, Wisconsin Danish kringle and bowls of fresh seedless fruit from Florida and Texas.

Gage, befitting his mood, stayed with black coffee and ignored the rest. He and his subordinates sat at a rectangular table of dark cherry, with Gage occupying the center section of the side facing the room's hallway entrance. Hawkins sat on his right, Stewart on his left. Across the table was Winston Marlowe, head of internet stuff, as Gage liked to say, Ben Levy, and Fielding Wallace III. Vicki Prentiss, the Eagle News TV journalist, and Dr. Mortimer Mullins, head of the economics department at Columbia University, sat on the ends. Behind

Gage were elegant glass doors offering a picturesque view of the White House Chrysanthemum Garden.

Low-volume, casual conversations suggested nothing was terribly urgent or important. When Gage set his cup down hard with a scowl on his face, the room fell obediently silent.

"There are a lot of people starving in this world," he began evenly, tapping his fingers lightly. "There are the sick, the homeless. Our freedom missions abroad are targeted by terrorists, which means around-the-clock warfare. Civilians, including children, spend their days and nights wondering whether they're going to be blown up. We have people over here who worry about them. Worry -- and lobby for more aid or to get us to pull our troops out. We have legions of Greens worldwide who want us all to take baths once a week instead of showers every day and who scream for the nationalization of the economy every time they feel a warm breeze . . . which is every day. We have floods, hurricanes, earthquakes, tornadoes, tidal waves . . . and the social fallout from each. We have Hollywood gossip, political corruption, and around the clock sex and blood on TV. Then we have sports, shopping, and religion breaking and entering into America's homes. We also have . . . What? I'm sure I'm forgetting something. . . This is how it's been for a long time. Do you agree?"

He looked around. Heads were nodding.

"So, tell me, how is it that—" Gage paused and closed his eyes, seeking self-control. "—*monetary theory* . . . has become a matter of public concern?"

His question was met by eager silence.

Vicki broke the spell. "What makes you think it has, Max? You see the usual articles about money in the financial press, but no more than normal."

"You're right," Gage said, "I didn't make myself clear. The financial crowd, they'll play any game you give them. Just tell them the rules. The clever ones will always figure out how to profit from it. And the academics -- they're an entity without reflexes. Give them a few years and a hundred conferences and maybe they'll acknowledge, in one of their quarterly journals, what's happening. So it isn't a hot issue with them, either."

He bent down and pulled a stack of papers off the floor, rose from his chair, and dropped the pile in the center of the table. It landed with a resounding *whump!* Regal china rattled. He remained standing.

"Commentary. Culled at random from numerous internet sites. People talking about what money is or should be." He grabbed pages off the pile and flung them in the air. "They're talking about the Fed as the power behind our wars. They're blaming central banks for poverty, the destruction of the family . . . the goddamn military-industrial-congressional complex . . ." He leaned in Wallace's direction, enunciating each syllable carefully: "They're blaming our inflation-fighter for the very thing it's fighting!" He straightened and looked around. His face was already starting to purple. "People who can't balance their goddamn checkbooks are mouthing off about fiat money as if they knew what the hell they were talking about."

"Sir—" Wallace began.

"Don't tell me about Preston Mathews. He was only a man. This is an abstract theory we're talking about. *An abstract theory!* No man in the history of the planet has ever gotten the average dope interested in abstractions. And this—" With a violent sweep of his hand he scattered the pile across the table. "—*this shouldn't be here!* Are you going to tell me the goddamn Fed chairman got it started with a couple of crazy stunts? Until yesterday's video at Morrisville, they had nothing in the way of mental tools to piece it together. Isn't that right, professor?" He turned to Mullins.

"There are no popular books on monetary theory, that's true," Mullins said. "Not yet, at least. And if someone picked up a textbook and worked their way through the section on money and banking, in all likelihood they would develop a deep respect for our system of money management." He added with a smirk: "If they didn't fall asleep first." There was a sprinkling of laughter, though Gage didn't crack a smile. "Really, Mr. President, notwithstanding your comments about academia's reflexes, we have watched with great curiosity the developments following the late chairman's demise, which looks increasingly like a martyred revolt on his part. Though I personally as well as most others who knew him thought highly of Preston Mathews, his attempt to revive the gold standard hasn't risen above the gutter. In other words, the authors of these screeds–" He picked up one of the pages and let it drop. "–are nothing. They're nobodies. Their stuff isn't peer-reviewed because they don't know what peers are. They're intellectual zeroes. They vocalize what stirs them, and what stirs them is envy – envy of the high and mighty. They have no political influence whatsoever. And though I haven't watched the video you mentioned, I see no cause for concern. Sir."

"If I may," Stewart said, getting a nod from Gage, "an analysis of the video shows strong similarities between the letter the mayor read and Mathews' writing style.  And she does claim he sent it to her."

"She's now a martyr among the unwashed," Levy added. "Imagine, an elected official attempting to blow the whistle on our wonderful monetary system.  Who the hell does she think she is?"

"We don't know when the video first appeared on barbarous-relic.com," Stewart continued, "but we did a quick take this morning and found seventy-seven other sites that were carrying it.  Some of those sites get a lot of traffic.  And a few already had favorable commentary on it.  Most of them carried a picture of Ward with blurbs declaring her to be a great hero.  Two of them said she was a hero in the war against government -- not *bad* government, which one site said was redundant -- *government*, period.  The blatant discrepancy between what the networks carried last night and what the video shows could come down on our heads."

"Since when do we worry about a bunch of internet anarchists?" Mullins said impatiently.  "If decent people are concerned about the discrepancy, tell them the letter read on the video was a complete fabrication – a skillfully-done hoax."

A brief pall of silence fell across the room, as if they had all suddenly become naked.

"Okay," Gage said as he seated himself.  "Granted, the issue is money, and money moves the world.  And the simplicity of the junk being written appeals to brains of few wires.  And of course the Fed chairman, the former one, is at the center of their warped universe, and now they've got his letter backing up some of their idiocies.  I know it's only the internet talking, but I don't like it.  And I want it stopped."  He took a sip of water and set the glass down.  "Permanently."

Winston Marlowe cleared his throat.  "I believe we have an answer for you, Mr. President," he said in a soft voice.

"No geek gibberish, doctor."

"Nor is any needed."  Marlowe was approaching fifty, with a frail build.  "Is there a major print publisher who doesn't know how politics is played?  Not to my knowledge. Is there a major electronic news producer who is indifferent to government reaction?  We all know the answer.  But the internet isn't called cyberspace for nothing.  It is out there in a world by itself.  Anyone can enter, anyone can leave.  And anyone can pretty much say what they want while they're out there.

"Alluding to Ms. Prentiss' comment, most Americans get their news from TV and talk radio and don't even know about the barn dollar or the Morrisville incidents.  All they know is Preston Mathews is gone and Dr. Wallace has replaced him. And most of them think Wallace has replaced him as Secretary of the Treasury.  That's right – people don't know the difference between the Treasury and the Federal Reserve. What's more, they don't care to know.  This is, perhaps, unfortunate, but it also has certain advantages for those seeking to preserve the status quo.  And most people, given the distractions you named, Mr. President, find the status quo acceptable.  It's the devil they know."

"—or think they know," Levy interrupted.

"True. But small movements have been known to gain strength without notice, and we would be unwise to ignore the events going on in cyberspace. In my own field I'm reminded of how an invincible mainframe giant was blindsided by an innocuous little desktop computer that could scarcely compute a month's average temperature, much less run a major corporation. This is not to say monetary theories pose a comparable threat. As we know, they're too abstract to be exciting. But because of the crucial importance of monetary control to . . . our way of working, we must treat the current situation as a threat to our existence, even though it has yet to invade the ranks of respectable commentary.

"Therefore, I propose a two-stage assault. We begin by plugging the hole in the dike. Dr. Mullins, I believe, has been approached about doing a layman's book on money."

Mullins was visibly annoyed. "Two graduate students have been in charge of putting it together, though I'll carry the byline. I didn't write a single word. This will absolutely be the nadir of my career."

"Well, the country thanks you for the sacrifice, nonetheless," Marlowe said. "I personally believe it will be a big hit. As the book makes its way through the ranks, we'll be moving into the second stage, which is to take control of cyberspace. We don't send cops out to shut down websites. We establish a way of surfing that makes cops unnecessary. We do that by imposing guidelines for website content.

"Does this sound too radical? If it does, allow me to remind you that the internet was originally a government creation. The internet owes its very existence to a 1958 Defense Department program called DARPA, out of which came a mainframe computer network called ARPANET, in 1969. The idea behind ARPANET was to allow researchers at four western U.S. universities to share information and operate other computers remotely using a communications paradigm known as packet switching. But true to human nature, people found it more interesting to swap news and personal messages than to share computing power.

"As parts of ARPANET became de-classified commercial networks began connecting to it. The physical structure of the network, what we call the trunk lines or backbone, were built, maintained, and financed by the National Science Foundation from the mid-1980s 'til 1994, when the backbone was privatized. ARPANET thus evolved into what we call the internet.

"In the mid-1990s, various governments around the world began restricting internet use. China, for example, requires all users and Internet Service Providers to register with the police. In Saudi Arabia, the public couldn't access the internet at all until 1999; access was originally restricted to universities and hospitals. In Singapore, if you manage a website that has religious or political content you must register with the state. So, my point is, we're hardly the first government to impose restrictions on internet access. And given that the internet began as a government program within the Department of Defense, I believe we have a responsibility to see that it's not used in a manner detrimental to the national interest."

Gage regarded the little man for a moment.

"So, doc," he said, "how the hell are we going to restrict access and get away with it?"

Marlowe smiled. "Give people a new browser."

## 13

Mort Mullins' ghostwritten *Monetary Theory for Patriots* hit the bookstores exactly three weeks later.

To the surprise of some, Mullins' doctoral students had not filled the book with slumber-inducing prose. Readers were greeted instead with characters from Andy Kline's popular comic strip *Pudding*, a world in which a motley collection of lost-and-found critters stumbled through life with a lovable tyrant called Rags.

Mullins spoke through Rags, whose job was to educate her normally wayward flock on the meaning of money and the reason we have a central bank that has sole responsibility for controlling the money supply. Rags' flock found her pronouncements fascinating and never once challenged them.

Most readers could get through the comic version of Mullins' ideas in a half-hour or less. The smart set thought it was cool to have Rags and her gang serving as a mouthpiece for one of the country's most eminent economists. As a bonus, they had the smug satisfaction of knowing they had digested a

Columbia professor's presentation of standard monetary theory, even if they were not altogether sure what he was talking about and were unaware of who actually wrote it.

With her troops seated cross-legged and gazing up at her in reverential awe, Rags summarized the fundamentals of the book on the last two pages. Hanging on the wall behind the kids was a sketch of the Rosenthal flag-raising on Iwo Jima.

First, said Mullins's-grad-students-through-Rags, money was crucially important to the general welfare of the American people. It was just as important as having a strong military or a sound educational system.

Second, because of this supreme importance, government has assumed responsibility for deciding what we should use for money and how much of it should be available. It was government's job to be in charge of, or at least regulate closely, things that affect us all, such as the military, schools, roads, the environment, the post office – and especially money. This is what the Constitution means by providing for the General Welfare. By controlling these things, the government is assuring us all a beneficent existence.

Third, since bankers were specialists in managing money, government long ago created a national organization of banks called the Federal Reserve System, whose job is to manage interest rate decisions through money supply accommodations. The Fed, as this organization is known, makes adjustments in the money supply to maintain the appropriate interest rate, which is the cost of borrowing money. The Fed prefers to keep interest rates as low as possible so that businesses will be encouraged to borrow and expand operations.  When businesses thrive, more and better jobs are available, and everyone prospers.

Fourth, the process by which the Fed adjusts the money supply is complicated and varies with the goal it's trying to reach.  In adjusting the money supply it normally works hand in hand with our federal government.  Usually the government starts the process by selling some of its bonds to the Fed.  The Fed pays for the bonds by writing a check that simultaneously creates the funds for it.  The check is deposited in a commercial bank where it is added to the bank's reserves for making loans.  Because businesses rarely have a need for physical dollars as such but rely instead on electronic transactions, banks are able to make loans safely beyond the amount of cash they have in reserve, a time-honored practice called fractional reserve banking.  In this way a million dollar bond purchase, for example, increases the money supply by one million dollars initially.  While holding ten percent of this amount in reserve, the banking system is able to create nine million dollars more in loans.

Fifth, and very importantly, the government needs our help in keeping the economy strong.  We should take advantage of the Fed's low interest rates by borrowing money for worthwhile things, such as vacations, houses, and sports utility vehicles.  As long as we can make our monthly payments we are helping the economy.  If we don't buy things on credit, or decide to hoard our cash in our homes instead of keeping it in government-insured banks or other financial institutions, jobs are lost and the economy suffers.

As a final wrap-up, Rags reminded readers that our monetary system is built on faith – faith in  government, the

Fed, business, and ourselves. We all need to keep paying our taxes and using credit wisely to make sure we have the jobs we want now and in the future. As with any faith-based endeavor, we should maintain an attitude of hope and humility. Given the complexity of managing interest rates in a vibrant modern economy such as ours, we should take every opportunity to support the president's choice for chairman of the Federal Reserve. With a huge wink at her obedient captives, Rags held up a mug shot of a smiling Dr. Fielding Wallace III, identifying him as the man President Gage had appointed as chairman because "he's a man who knows all about money and banking."

Reviews from the major media ranged from amused to glowing. None gave it a failing grade. Financial commentators generally praised it as a much-needed antidote to the mystery of the Fed, though with reservations about the book's attempt to simplify and make appealing something that is complicated and drab. Nonetheless, given its intended lay audience, they gave it high marks as a good starting place for understanding Fed operations. One reviewer wrote that "in bringing our banking system of fiduciary credit at long last into the sunlight for all to see, the book will send barbarous relic sympathizers scrambling for the cave from which they recently crawled."

Letters to book review editors – at least the ones that were printed – hailed the book as the Monetary Great Awakening. "The dollar is the offspring of the banking system and government," a sweet corn farmer from Palmyra, New York wrote. "And it's sound because it's based on the government's ability to pay its debts and on our ability to work and pay taxes. I can certainly live with that. The same interlocking system gives us the government we need as well as the money necessary to keep our economy growing. All my life I've wondered about those mysterious little bills I carry around in my wallet. Finally, someone has made it clear. Thank you, Mort Mullins and Rags!"

A reader from Butte suggested President Gage issue a directive making December 23 a national holiday in honor of the founding of the Fed in 1913. A woman from Detroit signing her letter "An FDR lover" suggested April 5 as a new holiday based on the president's declaration on that day in 1933 that severed our shackles to gold for all times. "It took a man of rare courage and vision to remove the major obstacle to the Fed's success, especially with many 'economists,' as they liked to think of themselves, urging him not to abandon the standard that was crippling our economy. I have no doubt whatsoever that God came back to earth as FDR to save us from the Depression created by the ravenous greed of unfettered capitalism, for which the gold standard was emblematic. One of the first things he did after inauguration was fix our bank and money problems. And not a quick fix, but a permanent one! I thank God now that Mort Mullins and his cartoon friends have explained these issues in a way that all people can understand and appreciate."

According to White House Chief of Staff Thomas Hawkins, President Gage ordered every member of his administration to read the book. It didn't take long for corporate CFOs to take the hint and insist all their top people learn Mullins' tale of the

Fed. A trickle-down effect kicked in and people everywhere were either reading the book or listening to Rags explain it on a downloadable audio file. Four weeks after publication it reached number one on the *Times'* list of nonfiction bestsellers.

14

*Political Plowshare*, the tabloid that feasted on politics, devoted a special issue to Mullins' book.

*Plowshare* featured a large picture of the *Money for Patriots* book on its front page, with a caption that read, "Cover for a massive fraud." When readers thumbed the page, perhaps expecting to find a scathing review inside, they were greeted instead with the following headline:

The Making of a Central Bank
John Law and the Mississippi Trading Company
France, 1716

Beneath this they found a narrative about John Law, the early eighteenth-century Scottish gambler and financier who thought the best way to revive an ailing economy was to remove the "scarcity of money," as he wrote in a 1705 monetary tract. A decade after its publication he took his ideas to the Continent and sold them to Philip II, the man in charge of France's finances, who needed a scheme more sophisticated than his failed program of coin clipping and confiscation to save the nation from bankruptcy.

In 1716 Phillip set Law up as head of the *Banque Générale*, the country's central bank, giving it and him monopoly control of the note issue. Having won the nation's trust with declarations of allegiance to sound money principles – he had promised his banknotes would be "payable on sight" in unadulterated gold coin – Law proceeded to apply another element of his theory. Because a scarcity of money, he believed, was the root of France's economic problems, and since banknotes backed purely by gold would be in short supply, he began issuing notes "backed" by the nation's vast landholdings. Exactly how one would redeem banknotes for acreage he neglected to explain.

Very importantly, Law and Phillip also created a trading company called the *Compaignie des Indes*, a vaporous entity said to have monopoly trading rights in France's Louisiana territory. Initially, shares in the company could only be purchased with government bonds still on the market, which had fallen to about one-fifth their value. To the public, the trading company and its investment strategy became known as the Mississippi System.

Phillip II was very pleased with the results. People from all ranks were buying shares of the *Compaignie des Indes*. Share prices began to soar. People were trading and speculating with Law's paper money, and France's economy was coming alive. Phillip decided John Law was correct that a shortage of money was an economic evil. He was so pleased with the change in the economy he brought government closer to the action. He renamed Law's bank the *Banque Royale* and by late 1719 had cranked out enough new bills to inflate the money supply by a factor of sixteen, no doubt to avert the evil of a monetary shortage. Thus, John Law, today regarded as the world's first central banker, had found a way to retire the government debt and provide the market with the elixir of virtually unlimited "liquidity."

What did this injection of "liquidity" do for the French economy? With unimaginable amounts of money pumped into the system, getting rich was unavoidable. Ordinary working people were becoming *millionaires*, a new term the aristocracy used with pejorative connotations. Shares sometimes rose 20 percent in a matter of hours. All one had to do was buy, hold, and sell to make a killing. As historian Charles Mackay noted, "many persons in the humbler walks of life, who had risen poor in the morning, went to bed in affluence." Law's coachman made enough money to buy a coach of his own and found Law a new driver. Law himself became the richest man in the world, owning, among other things, the central bank, the Louisiana Territory (roughly two-thirds of the present United States), a collection of French chateaux, and original works of masters such as Holbein, Michelangelo, da Vinci, and Rubens. He was so popular his carriage required a large military escort to protect him from admirers. As many of those admirers were women, some found ways to meet with Law despite the obstacles.

One day in early 1720 a certain aristocrat whom Law had offended, Prince de Conti, took his *Banque Royale* notes to the bank and presented them for redemption. The notes were reported to have filled three wagons. De Conti said something like, "Voila, monsieurs! Here are your notes, which are 'payable at sight.' Now, do you see them? Well then, hand over the coins."

The bank complied – and held its breath. On hearing about the exchange Phillip was so angered he ordered the prince to return two-thirds of the gold. De Conti obeyed grudgingly but in doing so triggered the first stirrings of panic. Soon two other aristocrats, motivated by distrust rather than revenge, came into the bank to begin presenting their notes in small quantities so as not to stampede the herd. Seeing a coming crisis, they hid their coins or shipped them to other countries for safekeeping.

Word got out, and Law's *Banque Royale* was challenged to prove its notes were as good as gold. They weren't, of course, and Law's hot air balloon burst. Common folk began storming the bank to pull their gold out. Like the aristocrats, they hoarded their money or shipped it somewhere safe to protect it from confiscation. With gold disappearing from the *Banque's* vaults, its notes no longer looked so trustworthy, and the money supply plummeted. In February 1720, in an effort to intimidate people into returning their gold to the *Banque*, Phillip declared "hoarding" a crime and threatened citizens with penalties if they were found with more than a pittance in coin. After that failed he tried tricking them into believing gold was going back to the *Banque* by printing over a billion livres worth of additional notes to pump up the money supply. As the final act of the tragic farce, John Law issued picks and shovels to the city's idlers and paraded them through the streets as heroes on their way to Louisiana to mine huge profits. It served only to underscore the fraud and the people's former credulousness. Law's "liquid" Garden of Eden evaporated into bankruptcy. Later that year Law left the country heavily in debt and died nine years later in Venice.

Is John Law regarded as a charlatan today? Alexander asked in his essay. Hardly. The most influential economists of modern times regard Law with sympathy and respect. One eminent economic historian places Law in the "front ranks of monetary theorists of all time." Others view him jealously for being the first economist to run an entire country, who thought it proper for government to issue paper money backed by promises, making him a forerunner of today's inflationists.

Alexander segued the narrative of Law with an excerpt from the Senate Banking Committee hearing, held three years earlier, on the nomination of Preston V. Mathews to be a member and Chairman of the Board of Governors of the Federal Reserve System.

Committee chair, Senator ALICIA MASON: Dr. Mathews, I commend you for your candor in our hearing today. As you may have noticed I take plenty of notes, and as I review my scribblings I see you have been refreshingly clear in your responses. For example, when committee members raised questions about how the Federal Reserve in its oversight capacity could allow so many banks to be undercapitalized, you didn't attempt to deny the problem, spread the blame, or liquidate the issue with slippery prose. You said it was "an alarming situation that signaled a serious failure of Federal Reserve oversight." Neither did you make any extravagant claims about the Fed's ability to manage the difficult goals of inflation and unemployment. "A sound monetary system is a necessary though not a sufficient condition of a prosperous economy," you said in a manner that reminds us you were once a college professor. Then you went on to add remarks about the Fed chairman's role as a commentator in general terms on issues outside his direct area of responsibility, particularly in the areas of government spending and deficits. You reminded us that the Fed is not economically omnipotent, and its policies are "frequently undermined by government extravagance." As I said, these answers and others, coming from a prospective Fed chairman, are refreshing and . . . perhaps a bit unsettling. Do you have any comments about that?

Dr. MATHEWS: People deserve straight answers when they ask honest questions, Senator.

Chairperson MASON: I certainly agree, but in the many hearings we have conducted in these quarters we have come to expect a mix of straight talk and the other kind, with emphasis decidedly on the latter.

Dr. MATHEWS: Other Fed chairmen have spoken of the need for more transparency in Fed operations. I agree with that cause and hope to further it significantly.

Chairperson MASON: Well, Dr. Mathews, let's see if you can advance the cause a bit more, shall we? A number of pundits have said the Federal Reserve is not the politically independent organization it pledges to be, and for that reason we will always be subject to inflation, unemployment, and recessions. How do you respond to this?

Dr. MATHEWS:  Senator, we need to acknowledge that the Federal Reserve System has political roots, inasmuch as the U.S. government created it with the Federal Reserve Act of 1913.  With the enormous regulatory environment we have today it is very difficult for any firm to be independent of politics, and even more so when the government is responsible for an organization's creation.

Chairperson MASON:  You're saying the Federal Reserve is not politically independent.  Are you also saying we're forever subject to the economic problems I named?

Dr. MATHEWS:  Not at all, though a look at the Fed's record for the first 70 years might suggest otherwise.

One of the Fed's jobs was to eliminate the crises that occasionally struck the economy prior to its inception.  It's also true that prior to the Fed's inception government intervened in the economy, our money and banking system included. Nevertheless, the national banks decided the existing system was too open and competitive and thus lobbied for more intervention.  From the mid-1890s, if not earlier, their goal was to win support for a central bank with a monopoly of the note issue and to serve as a lender that never ran dry.

The bankers needed government to make a central bank work – a free market precludes central banking.  Most people, of course, being staunchly pragmatic, don't care whether it does or not.  What they want to know is: How effective has the Fed been? When it began operations in 1914 the Comptroller of the Currency boasted that the new Federal Reserve "supplies a circulating medium absolutely safe" and will render financial and commercial crises such as occurred in 1873, 1893, and 1907 "mathematically impossible."  Was his statement true? Have we averted economic crises? Has the Fed preserved the value of the dollar?

[Mathews stands and reaches into his pants pocket.]

If you will, Senator . . . catch.

[He tosses a coin at Chairperson Mason. She claps it into her hands and looks at it. He takes his seat.]

You're holding in your hand a nickel, which is roughly what remains of the dollar since the Fed went to work. So much for the dollar as a store of value. As for economic crises, instead of identifying them by year, perhaps we should give them names like Camille or Katrina. They seem to occur at about the same frequency as killer storms, and both are generally regarded as beyond human control, as acts of God.

What do these facts say about our central bank?

Fed chairman Alan Greenspan is regarded by many people today as the greatest Fed chairman ever for steering the economy through several major crises. He's been knighted by the queen and awarded numerous honorary doctorates from some of the world's most prestigious universities.

In December 2002 he gave a speech to the Economics Club of New York that offered an interesting perspective on our country's monetary systems. In the 50 or so years following the abandonment of the gold standard in 1933, he said, prices rose by approximately 750 percent, as measured by the Consumer Price Index. The CPI, as it's called, is a basket of household goods that excludes certain items because of their volatility. He also noted the fact, startling to some, that in 1929 prices were about the same as they had been in 1800, though there were price fluctuations during that period. In other words, the gold standard held the line on prices over a 129-year period.  Throughout most of this period, as we know, the country experienced spectacular growth, rising real wages, and miniscule government debt.

But Mr. Greenspan's speech suggests another observation.  If we take his period and cut it off at 1912 instead of 1929 – 1912 of course being the year before the Fed was born – we find the CPI *falling* by roughly 57 percent.  Put another way, $19^{th}$ century Americans, whose dollars were defined as a weight of gold or silver, experienced falling prices and economic prosperity at the same time, a state of affairs we have a hard time even imagining today.

Let me say that again: Americans once understood falling prices and prosperity as natural bedfellows.  And the reason is quite simple.  In those days the production of goods and services outpaced the production of money.

So what happened after 1933 that drove prices through the roof?  Chairman Greenspan said:  "Monetary policy, unleashed from the constraint of domestic gold convertibility, had allowed a persistent overissuance of money."

The Fed's eager printing press could have led to our destruction, but fortunately it didn't.  "The adverse consequences of excessive money growth provoked a backlash," he said.  Beginning in 1979, the Federal Reserve, under new leadership and with the support of the government, "dramatically slowed the growth of money."  Consequently, we went through a sobering recession and the pace of inflation eased up.

Following this, the economy rebounded vigorously, and "the progress made in reducing inflation was largely preserved," Mr. Greenspan told his audience. "Although pressures for excess issuance of fiat money are chronic," he concluded, "a prudent monetary policy maintained over a protracted period can contain the forces of inflation."

In other words, when the Fed stops inflating, inflation stops.

But is this what Mr. Greenspan meant? Mr. Greenspan, you will remember, was famous for using words in such a way that no one was ever quite sure what he was talking about. For example, what did he mean by "contain the forces of inflation"? With little imagination it's possible to assign four or five meanings to that expression. And he used the words "*can* contain the forces," not "*would* contain" those forces. Nor did he say *how* the Fed would or could contain those forces, because we still operate without the constraint of gold convertibility.

But taking him in good faith, we assume he meant something positive, like "the Fed knows better than to push too hard on the peddle because we don't want another 'backlash.'" As long as the Fed has a backbone, with the will to resist the "excess issuance of fiat money," we'll stay out of trouble economically. So, while it makes no sense to talk of a political entity such as the Fed being politically independent, it makes a great deal of sense to talk of the determination of Fed officials to "just say no" when conditions warrant.

Chairperson MASON: You have some impressive notes at your disposal, Dr. Mathews. We all remember Mr. Greenspan, of course, but it's helpful to be refreshed on some of his comments. He had a fondness for gold.

Dr. MATHEWS: Yes, he did.

Chairperson MASON: In connection with your last comment – "just say no" – someone once wrote that gold says "no" a lot. Is that an expression you would agree with?

Dr. MATHEWS: It does say "no" because of its limited supply. Gold says "no" to a lot of bad ideas. It says "no" to deficit spending, which is precisely the reason it was ditched. As history makes clear, people in the twentieth century were sold on the idea of big government, so they needed a debt-based monetary unit to provide the "liquidity" needed to pay for it.

Fiat currencies have been very dangerous because there's no limit to their supply. They've also been very profitable to some people. Fiat currencies are monetary yes men and go along with just about anything. But saying "yes" has painful consequences, as Mr. Greenspan acknowledged. The nickel I tossed you is one of those consequences. If we allow ourselves to be taken in by "liquidity," as other countries have for over three centuries, it will be our downfall. But the United States is not just another country. As you're well-aware, we play a pivotal role in the global economy by virtue of the popularity of the American dollar. To a large extent it underpins the world economy. A dollar collapse, therefore, would have global consequences.

Chairperson MASON: Dr. Mathews, this "liquidity," what has it cost us in the past? Can you give us some examples? . . .

Alexander interrupted the hearing transcript with a visual presentation of his own creation:

A More Active Government

Sponsored in part by
Federal Reserve Liquidity

Beneath these words readers found pictures of twentieth century artifacts . . . a panoramic photo of the World War I Meuse-Argonne American Cemetery and Memorial in rural France, with its fastidious landscaping and row after row after row . . . after row . . . of white crosses, representing a portion of the young Americans killed to ensure victory for the Allies and thus keep them from defaulting on the massive loans J. P. Morgan had floated them with the aid of the new American central bank . . . a picture of an Edison stock ticker in meltdown from the panic selling on Black Tuesday . . . a crowd of people clamoring to get into a bank to claim the money they had left on deposit. Unknown to the depositors, the bank had loaned it to others . . . a picture of Franklin D. Roosevelt juxtaposed with an excerpt from his gold confiscation order of 1933, in which any Americans caught "hoarding" their gold became felons . . . a photo of a slaughtered pig, testifying to the government's economic wisdom of raising farm prices by reducing the food supply . . . a line of hungry men waiting to eat in a soup kitchen.

Further on he showed a U.S. Army photo of the mushroom cloud over Hiroshima . . . words and picture of a Korean "Police Action" veteran describing the effect of friendly-fire napalm dropped on his unit, in which American soldiers were burned so badly they were rolling in the snow begging to be shot as their skin hung like jerky from their faces, arms and legs . . . the Pulitzer prize photo of nine-year-old Kim Phuc

Phan Thi screaming and running naked down a road following an American-ordered napalm attack on her Vietnamese village . . . a picture of Nixon reassuring Americans in 1971 that " . . . your dollar will be worth just as much tomorrow as it is today," after announcing that the federal government would no longer honor its promise to foreigners to redeem their dollars for gold . . . and, finally, a government inflation calculator at http://www.bls.gov/ showing the dollar had lost eighty-five percent of its value since Nixon's promise.

The visual presentation ended with another excerpt from the hearing transcription:

Chairperson MASON: Do you have any closing comments, Dr. Mathews?

Dr. MATHEWS: Yes, thank you. I'm honored to have been nominated by the president and to be here today before such a distinguished committee. I've tried to be candid, and I hope you will take my candor in good faith. In my view, nothing is more important to our welfare than a healthy monetary system, and if confirmed I will do my best to see that we have one.

To underscore the meaning of Mathews' last sentence, Alexander provided them with another visual on the back cover.

It was an anonymous picture taken at night. The caption read, "He kept his word."

It was a shot Parks took without the FBI's knowledge and described to Nina on the morning of her visit to Preston's farm, showing the flaming wreck of the *Barbarous Relic* illuminating the Jolly Roger Dollar.

## 15

Shortly after Alexander's special issue hit the streets, a PDF version made its way to barbarous-relic.com. It also made its way to President Maxwell Gage after he delivered a stirring speech at a supporter's ranch in Texas to Veterans of Foreign Wars. The speech itself brought the usual ritual ovations for his boilerplate about the sacrifices required to defend freedom anywhere on the globe, but incredibly the loudest applause came when a wheelchair-bound old-timer suggested the last two letters of "VFW" were redundant since foreign wars were all anyone ever fought in. The questioner's tone sounded close to disdainful, which coupled with the applause was a shocking attitude from the amen corner. Gage joked his way out of it but left the ranch with his gut rolling.

His evening got worse on the flight back to Washington. In the calm surroundings of the presidential air fortress, Hawkins leaped up suddenly and body-slammed his laptop against the floor as if trying to kill a particularly tough insect, augmenting his actions with a burst of obscenities. He bolted from his seat and disappeared. Stewart had received the same email as Hawkins that linked him to the Plowshare special edition on barbarous-relic.com, but instead of exploding he read it with fascination. Gage ordered him to read it aloud then later told him to stop when he got to the part about American napalm turning GI's to jerky.

Two days later Winston Marlowe came to Gage and put him at ease. Nuisance variables like barbarous-relic.com would soon be history, he assured his president, because Stage Two of his plan was nearing completion. No state charged with defending the freedom and prosperity of its citizens should tolerate anything that interfered with its mission. It would be tolerating one's destroyers, he insisted. In the past, states had always watched activist anarchists closely and when necessary eradicated them, though with the usual nitpicking from malcontents about violations of inalienable rights. With Marlowe's plan there would be no need to get rid of anarchists because there would be no way for them to be heard.

For weeks, Marlowe had been testing a new browser in a former office equipment storage room in the basement of the White House. Marlowe's testers were teenage male technophiles. Per their job descriptions, most of their time was spent trying to access unauthorized internet sites. They were paid twice the federal minimum wage, given time off from school and limousine service from and to their homes, allowed to have all the snacks they wanted free, and given splotched red, white, and blue T-shirts they were encouraged to wear on the job. Working in the White House on a secret "freedom mission" while dressed in a free T-shirt was way cool.

Marlowe told them when their testing was complete they would be invited to join the president on-camera as he introduced the browser to the country as part of his Knowledge is Freedom program. "The president thinks of you seven lads as the Mag Seven," Marlowe added. "You know, short for Magnificent Seven . . . the movie." He had hoped the flattery would have a more conspicuous impact, but all he saw were a few simpers. He wasn't surprised, really. As a nerd himself for most of his life, his biggest challenge had always been to meet social expectations. Had they reacted like jocks to a pep talk he would have been alarmed.

His one concern wasn't their ability to do the assigned job, it was their potential to do much more. It was a reasonable risk, he believed, because he and other insiders, including Hawkins, would be testing the browser on their own. Plus the boys had no authority to change the browser, only to report problems directly to Marlowe. He told them nothing about the browser's software developer, nor did he give the developer any information about them.

They had been picked to win the confidence of the American public. Marlowe was certain that with proper management they would be up to the task.

## 16

Vicki Prentiss's biannual TV special came on the air at 7:30 p.m. to upbeat theme music.  She and her guests were seated in a circle open at one end.  It was an elegantly simple set – anything fancier might've detracted from the hostess, Eagle's 14-carot centerpiece.  As the camera moved in for a close-up, she greeted her viewers with an exuberant smile that no doubt took many of them prisoner.

"Hi, I'm Vicki Prentiss, and welcome to the second edition of 'The Browns versus the Dollar.'  For those of you who missed our inaugural broadcast six months ago, this is a program that tries to take the mystery out of inflation and present real-world ways of dealing with it without becoming an investment expert, assuming there is such a person.

"Tonight we're going to hear how the Browns – as we refer to these six people – have been doing since our last show.  'The Browns versus the dollar.'  You're all familiar with the dollar.  Let's meet the Browns.  They are, on my left, Mr. Binkowski, Mr. Robeson, and Mr. Ortega.  And on my right, Ms. Wright,

Mr. Nguyen, and Mr. Sanders. Welcome back, guys. Good to have you here. Tell me, how's life been for you folks since becoming the team facing the declining dollar?"

"A day doesn't pass without receiving an offer to borrow," Mr. Ortega said.

"You're getting more offers than before?"

"Even my father-in-law has offered to lend me money. Creditors see me as riskproof. They think Uncle Sam is secretly underwriting my success."

"Because you're a famous Brown now."

Ortega chuckled. "Yeah."

"What's funny?"

"Some of my friends are calling me Brown. José 'Brown'?" He shook his head.

"Do you agree with the creditors? Do you think you're a no-risk borrower?"

"We've all thought about it, I'm sure. I could go borrow $100,000 and find out."

"Are you tempted?"

"*I'm* not. Can't say the same for others in my family. They see it as free money."

"So you're under pressure to borrow more – and not just from creditors."

"The creditors are easy. Telling my family 'No' is a different matter."

"How about the rest of you? Do you find the credit offers tempting?"

"How else are you going to be a good American?" Ms. Wright said. "The president tells us spending is good for the economy. Once upon a time the government wanted us to be savers. Now it's patriotic to be buried in debt."

"That's right, lady," Mr. Robeson interrupted. "And if all that debt is causing you sleepless nights, listen to the Battle Hymn while you're falling asleep, you'll nod off in no time. You know"—he broke into a crude baritone—'Mine eyes have seen the glory of the coming of high debt.' You've gotta be creative. Patriotic music – it'll keep all your fears at bay. You won't worry about your bills. Or the wars. Or the economy. Or—"

"—I think it comes down to using good sense," Vicki said to forestall more cynicism. "We need—"

"—But maybe it's true," Robeson said. "Maybe Gage won't let us fail. Does anyone have the number of the White House? We need a clarification. He could turn this show into a Wall Street bonus party."

"Why don't you do that for us, Mr. R?" Vicki said without fracturing her light mood. "But on your own time, if you will. We don't have the minutes to spare. Let me ask you – Mr. B – how are you doing overall? Better than six months ago? About the same? Don't know?"

"My mother lives on a fixed income," Binkowski said, "and she was having a hard time getting by. We're helping her out now. So that's taken a toll."

"What a good son *you* are," Vicki said. "Aren't you fortunate you're able to do that."

"Let's see," Robeson said, "bailing out Mom after she spent herself into a deep hole. Is that part of the CPI?"

"Hey, my mom saved every cent she could spare! She didn't even own a TV until we bought her one three years ago."

"You bought her a TV and now you're supplementing her income? Wow, Bink, sounds like you've got this inflation stuff whipped. It must be nice living in hog heaven."

"Yeah, 'hog' is right," Binkowski said. "A hog on the conveyer belt."

"Mr. Nguyen, you look very content," Vicki said. "Do you have good things to report?"

"We buy new home, you see," Mr. N began. "Bank want no money . . . uh . . . no money . . ."

"No money down?"

"No money down. We pay twenty thousand dollar."

"You put twenty thousand dollars down on a new house?! Good for you."

"Better for relatives. They move in. Driveway full of cars. They park in street, on lawn. Neighbors don't like."

"Are your relatives out of work? What's the deal with them?"

"They work, then spend money. No save. Leave housing to us."

"Couldn't they get an offer like yours? No money down?"

"Yes." He shrugged. "Other things come first. Nothing happen."

"It must be awfully difficult with your relatives living with you. It would be for most people."

Nguyen smiled. "American dream turn into Asian nightmare."

"Well, maybe they'll assist you financially later in life, as Mr. Binkowski is doing with his mother."

"I throw them out next month."

"Oh."

"I give them money. What you say? 'They swim or sink'?"

"Well, if they put it towards a house maybe it'll help you and the market. As the president tells us, we need to keep borrowing and spending to keep the economy strong." She turned to another Brown. "Mr. Sanders. I understand these are stressful times for you, as well, but you still agreed to be on the show. We very much appreciate that. Divorce is another one of those things that doesn't reflect in inflation indexes."

"We're separated at the moment. We've sold our house . . . at below-market value. She moved in with a girlfriend. I'm living in a small condo."

"You have no children, is that correct?"

"Right."

"Tell us a little more about your situation, if you will."

"Before our marriage we had talked about raising a family, but now she doesn't want to stay home and do the raising. She's a supervisor with a promising future. I'm a project engineer at a transonic wind tunnel."

"Do you believe you could raise a family comfortably on your income?"

"I thought so. We test a lot of military aircraft, so I'm putting in a lot of overtime. But she pointed out that my field is subject to violent employment instability. When the work slows, we get laid off."

"What field is she in?"

"IT. She travels to Japan twice a year and does other traveling as well. She finds it exhilarating. Raising kids is no longer in her crystal ball."

"And you didn't want to be Mister Mom and stay home with them?"

"I thought about it. For a few minutes." The others laughed. "But it was pointless. She didn't want to go through a pregnancy and miss work."

"So, it's really hard to compare your cost of living now to when you were both living under the same roof."

"I haven't given it much thought, with moving and everything. I know I'm not doing as well. But I have a plan. I have an MBA in finance along with my engineering degree. I'm setting my sights on Wall Street."

"Finance? How long have you been working as an engineer?"

"Six years."

"And you want to find work on Wall Street? Is that where your heart is now?"

"No. That's where the money is now."

"But the bubble can pop on Wall Street, just like in aerospace engineering."

"Yes, but on Wall Street you're in a better position to see the pop coming."

She sighed. "Well, folks, I thought you'd all come armed with spreadsheets showing cost comparisons of everyday items. This is turning into a soap opera." She laughed. "I'm okay with it as long as you are. This is real life. "

"We don't need spreadsheets to tell us things are costing us more," Ortega added.

"That depends on your income, though," Vicki said. "If you live in flatland, every price increase brings you closer to poverty, or deeper into it if you're already there. Otherwise, it's a race. There are strategies for winning that race. Have we heard any here?"

"Absolutely," Robeson said. "Sanders is moving to where the new money first lands. If he's sharp he'll make so much in commissions he won't have to worry about inflation, unless worst-case strikes."

"Worst-case?"

"Runaway inflation. But since all the leading experts assure us it can't happen here, he has nothing to worry about. And Mr. Nguyen is booting his relatives out. That'll save him money, unless they boomerang back. No offense, Bink, but you won't be supporting your mom forever. In the meantime you should have a hefty tax write-off. And since the government's into managing the population like a herd of sheep, it might consider outlawing divorce. People who are married will be forced to stay that way under penalty of law, and since most couples work, that'll keep them treading water longer. It'll also mean more money for government in tax receipts. Of course, if Gage is backing the six of us, that's the best strategy. We'll have the printing presses working *for* us instead of against us."

"I trust if that impossible case should somehow come to pass, at least you, Mr. Robeson, will tell us about it."

"I'll come by in my new Maserati and tell you personally."

"I'm sure you will. I'm almost afraid to ask, but how have you been doing? Are you staying ahead of the price increases?"

"I am now. I was a store clerk and attending college. I was working on a dream, wanted to be an architect – you know, a career with hard work, but *satisfying* hard work, because I'd be designing buildings. Then during break from school I took a trip to Vegas and joined a card game. I cleaned up. I mean, I cleaned UP, baby! At first I thought, I can pay for college now. Then I thought, Why bother? So, that's my job, playing cards. People think I'm very lucky. I'm not. I just know how to win at cards."

"You've figured out how to beat Vegas?"

"No. I don't play Vegas. I play where I can win."

"It sounds almost like you cheat."

"I do not cheat. I want that made clear – I do not cheat. There's a science to poker if you're willing to spend the time to learn it."

"Do you stay out of debt?"

"Sure. But I won't if Gage and his banker buddies come through. I'll see you in my Maserati if he does."

"If there's one thing I can guarantee, it's that no one will be bailing any of you out for debts you can't pay – no one in government, at least. Yes, you're all quite visible, but for that reason alone there can be no official offers of help. It simply wouldn't be fair to the millions of other people who need help with their loans."

"The Fed bails out big banks," Robeson said. "Why not us?"

"Because they're big, okay? And a big bank means a lot of depositors would get hurt if it went under."

"So if we had six million people sitting around here instead of six, chances are Gage would come through."

"I don't know, Mr. Robeson. I just don't know."

"Especially if those six million were voters from key states," Mr. Binkowski added.

"Let's return to our more humble goal of trying to deal with everyday price increases, shall we?" Vicki suggested, her demeanor showing the first signs of wilting. "I don't claim to understand the government's ways. They do things that sound okay at first, like bail out a big bank, but if you probe a little deeper you dig up . . . problems. We're not here to analyze the government, however. We're here to learn better methods of surviving in an inflationary economy."

"What if the inflationary economy is government's doing," Robeson asked, "even if it's done indirectly through its central bank?"

"The government would have no reason to do anything that would force prices up. That's absurd. The central bank is viewed by every reputable economist as the nation's premiere inflation *fighter*. Mr. R . . . please, let's move on."

"Gotcha," Robeson said.

"Many families rely on two incomes as an inflation strategy," Vicki continued, "though often without realizing it's a strategy for fighting inflation. But the two-income approach has its limitations, too. Not only is it sometimes temporary, as when couples split up, but in many cases it simply isn't an option. Ms. Wright, it's not a choice you have at the moment, correct?"

"Correct."

"Yet I understand you have an approach that's quite effective, even if old-fashioned."

"I guess you're talking about my promotion."

"Has it helped?"

Ms. Wright laughed. "It has. But it hasn't helped *me*," she said.

"I don't understand. They're paying you more money. How could it not help you?"

"My tax bite is bigger, and everywhere I turn I see a bill. I'm now the official guardian of my son's kids."

"My goodness! And your son . . .?"

"Oh, he's in jail again. Caught doing drugs. Even if he wasn't in jail I wouldn't want his kids raised in the kind of company he keeps."

"Just so our viewers know, you're a divorced mom, is that right?"

"Yes."

"And you work as a . . ."

"As an executive assistant in a big company."

"And your son's kids are how old?"

"The boys are eight, eleven, and thirteen."

"Three boys! Do you have any help raising them? What about the boys' mother? Where's she?"

"In and out of drug rehab. She can't take care of herself, let alone three kids. I'm thinking of getting some help. I can't do it alone, it's a second full-time job."

"And when you do get help, up go the expenses even more."

"That's the way it works."

"I can't . . . I just . . . I mean, how do you come home every night and deal with three young boys . . . by yourself?"

"You don't ask how. You just do it."

"You're still a reasonably young woman. What does this do for your social life?"

Ms. Wright laughed.

"Okay, dumb question."

Vicki paused for a moment to preface a serious comment.

"We need to break shortly for messages, but before we do, let's ask: what can we make of all this? I see several things. First, no one here is on easy street, not even you, Mr. R. You might be today, but games can be won or lost, and you could lose. Second, prices are hurting the elderly on fixed incomes, but they're also hurting those who care for them, since their costs are going up. And with people living longer, that's no small consideration. Third, cheap credit effectively outlaws savings, and savings have traditionally, at least, been the source of our prosperity. Today, instead of using savings, banks are buying government debt and using that for money. Debt is money – government debt, that is. Not your debt or mine. How debt replaced gold and silver as money is a mystery to me, but that's what happened. The result of debt-based money is lower interest rates, which attract borrowers and discourage savers. People have money to spend but they're not savers, they're borrowers. The difference is, borrowers haven't earned their money yet. We have to ask what this . . . monetary policy does to our culture. Is cheap credit promoting the idea of a free lunch? 'Everything's free in America,' so the Broadway song goes. Everything – including wars? It takes time for savings to accumulate. But the longer people hold onto their money, the less it is worth. So where's the incentive to save? Where's the incentive to work to accumulate savings? It's not there. It's not there because of all the cheap credit. Who's responsible for cheap credit?

"And more disturbing still, why do we live under a system like this? Americans are not stupid people. It must benefit somebody. The question is, who?"

## 17

"I'm going to blow up Washington," Nina fumed to Greg Reece as she met him coming down the hall towards her. Reece smiled. "About face," she directed.

"What now?" he asked as they walked together.

"Orders from on high. We're supposed to devote more time to teaching the theories outlined in a popular comic book and less time on free market money and banking. Otherwise, we're quote, failing to prepare our students for the real world, unquote."

"How high were the orders' point of origin?"

"The board. Our honorable department head served as messenger. Keefe says foundation grant money's at stake. Or will be."

"So, what are your new guidelines? How much time is enough?"

She didn't answer. They were passing her secretary's desk and coming into her office. She dropped into her high-back chair and rubbed her temples. He sat on the edge of a table piled with papers and books.

"We have no guidelines," she said in a strange high voice. "No, that's not true. We're all grown up and expected to know how the game is played. So our guidelines are to ditch free market perspectives and preach central banking and fiat money exclusively. *Exclusively.*"

"You're constitutionally incapable."

"Oh? I used to think the same of my former husband. He became the enemy's top gun. I have to be practical, Reece. I have a fairly prestigious job that pays enough to keep me from night work. You think I'm going to blow a deal like this over a technicality like money and banking theories?"

"I'd bet my life on it."

She sighed. "I tried to explain to Keefe that we've always taught the gospel of Mullins and his kind in contrast to free markets and sound money, with emphasis on the latter. Apparently, economics is a government activity now, from paper money to quantifiable aggregates, and any mention of people engaging in voluntary exchange without state oversight is no longer even regarded as quaint. It's pure heresy."

"Have you thought about a petition?"

"Yeah, and so has Keefe. He said it would be treated as a letter of resignation for each of the signers. If we're willing to compromise we can encourage government to be more responsible in its regulations and control. Begging the state for more freedom, with hat in hand, is quite acceptable. In the academic community that's considered responsible freedom fighting. Really, our only restrictions are calling for a significant cut in Leviathan's size. That would weaken the power of government, and we are never to take that approach. We are not permitted to step outside the clutches of our masters. In case you're wondering, these are my words, not his. Can we still call for the abolition of the Fed? Sure. Of course we can. *Absolutely.* As long as we recommend a new monopoly to replace it."

"Like all those replacements for the income tax. God, Nina. I'll be flipping burgers for the rest of my life."

"That's the second-most cynical comment I've heard so far. The first came from Norton, who suggested we apply for redefinition as classicists and teach free markets as part of Western mythology."

"Better that than shills for the state."

**18**

The big night had arrived, and Gage was almost giddy with anticipation.  If the rumors he had heard were any indication, he would soon be likened to Franklin Roosevelt at one of his fireside chats.  There were problems with the country, and it was government's job to fix them.  Tonight Gage would be chatting with his neighbors across the land on national TV, letting them know how government was going to make their lives better.  People trusted informality, and a strong dose of high energy would help, too.  Instead of a fireplace he had all-pro quarterback Danny Flynn.  He and Flynn were tossing a football around on the set.

This was a bold move for a presidential address.  Tonight there would be no polished desk in the Oval Office.  Tonight he would be speaking from the test site for the government browser, a former storeroom that still retained much of its blandness.  The flag was there but so were seven workstations and seven teenage boys, each wearing their freshly-laundered

red-white-and-blue T-shirts and jeans. They were doing things at their computers, exactly what no one cared. Hawkins had simply told them to look busy. The President of the United States, instead of sitting at a desk in a hand-tailored suit, was scurrying around in front of the testers playing catch, wearing a Navy-blue turtleneck and slacks, both items imported from China.

It occurred to Gage that they should have called this The Preston Mathews Show, since the former Fed chief had made it possible. But then he would've felt obliged to trace the connections from Mathews' stunts to the new browser, and that might have weakened his position considerably. A broad smile creased his face as he drew his arm back to flip the ball to a loping Flynn. Tonight's announcement would be a landmark moment in his administration.

He sent the ball sailing, and it seemed destined to conk a technician on the back of his head until Flynn lunged and snagged it with one hand. "Don't make me look too good, Danny," Gage called out. "Someone might think I was in the wrong job."

"As the saying goes, Mr. President," Flynn called out, "those who can, do; those who can't, run the country."

"Have that man audited!" Gage called out in mock seriousness. He chuckled to cover his sudden doubts about Stewart's selection. Was Flynn one of his boys, as Stewart said he was? Flynn smiled and zipped a spiral back to Gage effortlessly.

"Three minutes to air time," a young woman announced from behind the cameras.

"Good evening, my fellow Americans."

Gage began on cue, looking almost dashing in his casuals. He stood in front of the Mag Seven. "I hope you'll forgive me for breaking with tradition this once as I speak to you from our White House test site. Tonight I wish to address a subject of major importance to all of us: the internet. But first . . . pardon me for one moment. Someone has issued a challenge."

Flynn stepped out in front of the camera holding the football. He turned and beamed a movie star's smile to the viewers. Gage welcomed him in grand fashion. "All-pro quarterback, Danny Flynn, ladies and gentlemen."

"Don't drop the ball, Mr. President," Flynn said, tossing Gage an easy spiral. Gage watched the ball into his hands and squeezed it. He held it up triumphantly. The computer kids behind them manufactured enthused cheering, as did the TV crew. "That's what I call a catch under pressure," Flynn added.

Gage underhanded the ball back to him with a sweeping movement of his arm. "Good luck next season, Danny." Flynn left the scene with a wave and another flash of ivory.

"Many of us enjoy football as we also enjoy the internet," Gage told the viewers. "They're both great American pastimes. And we wish to keep them that way.

"Unfortunately, the internet has suffered from a problem that plagues all freestyle enterprises. Most of what it offers is innocuous, helpful, or fun, but some of it exceeds what are generally regarded as common standards of decency. Football without established rules wouldn't be fun to play or watch. So it is with web surfing.

"Up to now the internet has existed in a state of anarchy, a condition fundamentally at odds with our American sensibilities. We Americans love our freedom and are always willing to fight for it, but we don't tolerate lawlessness.

"Tonight, therefore, I am announcing a new way of internet surfing that will eliminate the problems we've been experiencing while retaining our cherished American ideals. Working with some of the country's top software professionals, my administration has developed a new internet browser that will enforce a commonly accepted set of rules on our surfing experience. We call it, appropriately, the Liberty Browser. Many Americans have contributed their valuable time in making the Liberty Browser a success, but none more so than the seven young men behind me, who because of their technical brilliance I think of as the Mag Seven. Through their unrelenting efforts they have certified that the Liberty Browser works as designed."

He turned to the boys with an open hand of gratitude. "Thank you, men." They waved back with smiles that concealed neither their intelligence nor their love of mischief. Gage moved away from them to a safer background: an unoccupied workstation centered between the American flag and the U.N. flag hanging from poles.

"They've had the Liberty Browser on their minds constantly these past six weeks, and quite frankly I wouldn't want it any other way with something this important. But they're more than computer wizards. These young men are in agreement with me that all Americans are entitled to a healthy, robust computing environment. Now, what does this mean? It means a computing experience untarnished by pornography.

It means no more sites explaining how to make an atom bomb. It means no more chat rooms where pedophiles can snare innocent children. No more forums where atheists can spew their hatred of our religious values. No more websites that are the equivalent of someone crying 'fire!' in a crowded theater. The American internet user should be able to surf all he or she wants and never encounter anything that undermines the safety, morals, or prosperity of the American people.

"Now, one of the first questions you ask of a program called the Liberty Browser is how does it deal with controversial information? Let me assure you, all of my favorite critics will be alive and well under the auspices of the Liberty Browser. Responsible criticism of your government, in other words, will continue to flourish, as it should in a free nation such as ours.

"Another reasonable question to ask is how will the Liberty Browser program be paid for? In addition to the cost of software development and testing, we will need additional personnel to administer website authentication and supervision. But instead of asking for a tax increase, we decided to use the same financial model for web surfing that we use for our educational system. In other words, the Liberty Browser and its support are a government-guaranteed entitlement. And to underscore this point, I'm asking Congress for an across-the-board tax cut. No matter which income bracket you're in, you can look forward to a pro rata decrease in the amount of your annual liability. . ."

The following morning's Establishment commentary gushed with praise over Gage's announcement. "Americans have always recognized anarchy as the enemy of liberty," one scribe wrote. "The cliché 'freedom isn't free' is true. If people want freedom, they have to pay for it with restrictions and sacrifice. Finally, we will have a browser that will enforce our American ideals, as the president stated. And to put a pretty face on it, the browser comes packaged with a tax cut. Who in their right mind could ask for anything more?"

Another writer pointed out that "the browser wars have been a clear example of the harm caused by unbridled competition. Commercial browsers have so many security holes identity theft has become a booming business, while on the other end competition is so cutthroat browser developers are giving their products away. Liberty Browser will bring peace to the scene."

Only Terry Parks of the *Times* stepped away from the pack:

> Last night President Maxwell Gage announced a New Freedom for web surfers in the form of a purposeful collection of government bytes called the Liberty Browser. Though the identities of the browser's developers remain unknown, viewers across the land were shown the seven lads who played a vital role in testing it, none of whom looked old enough to vote. Since young males are at the bleeding edge of new technology, their presence on the show was apparently intended as reassurance that all is well with surfing under the American democratic state. If things go as

planned, the Liberty Browser will be the true legacy of Preston Mathews, rather than his infamous pirate dollar.

President Gage did not mention Mathews on his show, of course, but it is well-known among the media that Administration officials have been very disturbed over the popularity of a website known as barbarous-relic.com, the contents of which have been reproduced on other sites and blogs and which has generated a cult following among the T-shirt and tattoo crowd. One reaction to the barbarous relic's surging popularity still sits atop the *Times* bestseller list for nonfiction. Not content with winning such a strategic victory in the realm of ideas, our government has turned to its specialty to see that all competing theories are eased out and no new ones arise.

Seems the president forgot to mention that the Liberty Browser is a stand-alone application. It stands alone, meaning it has no competition. In a very short time, all other browsers will fall into oblivion. By government decree. Liberty Browser is just like Mathews' former employer, the Federal Reserve. It has no competition, either, by government decree.

Furthermore, the Liberty Browser will only recognize sites that have been approved by the government, much like the only drugs we can legally obtain are those approved by the Food and Drug Administration. Though President Gage assured us that all his "favorite critics would be alive and well" under the Liberty Browser, we need to consider what that might mean.  Certainly his "favorite" critics are not those exposing the Federal Reserve's spurious underbelly in web-only commentary.  And what if one of his "favorite" critics, such as the present writer, should happen to fall out of favor, on the occasion, perhaps, that someone in the Gage administration reads today's column?  Will I be sent to some government school to get my thinking straight, or will I simply disappear into the night?

But fear not.  Liberty is preserved.  If you hold radical views on the government you'll still be able to express them, as long as you do it in shower stalls with the water running hard.  And who can complain about the price?  We're getting something for less than nothing, a trick only government and its inscrutable methods of financing can get away with.

What we're seeing with the internet is what happens to all major industries as they mature.  They require a government full nelson to make sure the public gets what it deserves.

**19**

She passed the New Day DUI school, the Oriole Pawn Emporium, Lovejoy's package store, and a couple of joints that looked like girlie bars -- Life After Work and The Party's Here -- before arriving at her destination, a faceless one-story warehouse with weeds poking through cracks in the parking lot. She had never been to Silver Spring before but had always heard it was upscale. This, obviously, was the part she hadn't heard about. She parked as close as she could to the entrance and looked around carefully before stepping out of her Sentra. She was wearing a beige Hilfiger sweatshirt and jeans and felt overdressed. A heavy steel handrail led her up the concrete steps and hooked a right to the door, which was apparently built to withstand runaway trucks and other comparable shocks. A sign over the entrance read:

*Welcome to Potomac Plowshare*
*All the dirt they'd rather we not print.*

She went inside, carrying an optical disk jewel case in her hand.

"Look at me!" Scott Alexander shouted at her from across the room, as she gazed at the open pit of cubicles. Alexander, tall and lean and still under forty with a shock of full red hair, stood at the threshold of the one office in the area. Almost everyone in the cubes was on the phone or typing into a computer or both. From what she could see they were all women, and all reasonably attractive. "My mother wanted me to be a doctor and serve humanity," Alexander boomed. "How's this for a close second?"

"Mr. Alexander?" she asked.

"The name's Scott. What's up?"

"I have something for you to print." She held the jewel case up. "An unpublished book by Preston Mathews."

Heads turned and hands fell idle. The room got very quiet.

"Where did you get it?" Alexander asked in a softer voice.

"A friend who wishes to remain anonymous."

"A mystery! I love mysteries, at least the ones I can solve. You look familiar. Do I know you?"

She smiled. "No, we've never met."

"Well, then, let's meet. Step over here."

Alexander's eyes flew over the blocks of words that flicked onto his LCD monitor with every press of the page-down key. The monitor sat on the left side of his desk, affording him a view of his visitor sitting in front of it, had he wished to turn his head in her direction. She was intrigued by the speed with which he soaked up the material.

He looked at her. "Your friend suggested you bring this to me to publish. Do you know what we publish?"

"Dirt."

"Correct." He resumed reading but at a slower pace.

He stopped and looked at her again. "Do you know the difference between dirt and dynamite? No, you wouldn't, you're too young. *This* is beyond dirt. This is dynamite. We don't publish dynamite. People won't read it. But they will read dirt."

She shifted in her seat. "Well, I--"

"What's the difference between dirt and dynamite? Dirt exposes corruption in a system believed to be sound. Dynamite exposes the system as fundamentally unsound. The first calls for cleaning up the system. The second calls for throwing it out. People don't like to have systems they're dependent on thrown out, unless they see a better deal in the offering. And they never, ever, ever consider 'freedom' a better deal. You seem tense. Get *really* tense."

An embarrassed smile lit up her face.

"If we published dynamite, and the dynamite did its job, there would eventually be no dirt to publish, and we'd find ourselves out of a job, wouldn't we? So we publish dirt, not dynamite. This is dynamite. In the three-plus years this rag has been in existence we have never published dynamite. It's also true no one's ever submitted any dynamite to publish. You're asking me to break a sacred editorial standard."

"Do you know . . . who might be interested in publishing it?"

"Damn right I do – me! When the dynamiter is the former money czar, people will read it. Or they'll try. Or they'll stick their nose in it. They won't ignore – you're the girl on BRC! What's your name?"

She blushed some more. "I'd rather not say, if you don't mind."

"I don't mind. You deal in contraband. I'd want to be anonymous, too."

"Thanks." She looked at the floor, suppressing a smile.

"Your face is telling me something. What is it?"

"People I associate with call me Barbie. Barbie Relic."

He took a moment to remind himself what an attractive girl she was. "Barbie," he said simply.

"It's not my real name."

"You and your made-up name are the perfect match."

"Thanks."

"Well, I'm honored to meet you, Barbie, and you have my solemn word that I will dream about you tonight. You do know that barbarous-relic.com is going away, along with every other site that's a hot poker up the fat behinds of the politicos? Excuse my language. Including *my* sacred site. But you have a great deal of potential if you're a friend of BRC. Are you pleased I recognized you?"

Her cheeks dimpled into a smile. "Yes."

"How did you and BRC become buddies?"

"I answered an ad on the internet. They were looking for someone to help promote their website."

"Smart move. Is Preston Mathews alive?"

The question landed with its foot out, hoping to trip one of hers. "Well, . . . wasn't he . . . killed in a plane crash?"

"I don't know. Does your friend know if he's alive?"

"Mr. Alexander, please . . ."

He stood up at his desk and lurched at her. "Preston Mathews is *alive?!*"

"*I didn't say that!*"

He plopped down in his chair. "You didn't, that's true. But I need to know who to pay for this." He nodded at the computer monitor.

"You don't have to pay anyone. It's a donation."

"And Preston Mathews is the donor?"

"I suppose . . . since he's the author . . ." She blushed.

"The author who wrote this before his fateful flight."

"Right."

"Because dead men make lousy writers."

"I'm sorry," she said, "I can't help you."

He leaned back in his chair. "But you have. Immensely. Ever hear the question about a tree falling in the forest? If it falls, and no one's there to hear it, does it make any noise? That's a stupid question in science but a profound one otherwise. If a man tells a woman he loves her but she doesn't hear him say it – you get my point. Barbie, please tell your anonymous friend that with more gratitude than I can possibly show I will publish his book – or this book, if your friend is not Mathews. I will publish it immediately. It will shock the publishing world though probably not the rest of the planet. I will publish it, and it will explode, but I'm not sure if it will make any noise."

## 20

" . . . The government has given us this," Lisa-as-Barbie continued, holding up a copy of Mullins' book. Behind her was a photo enlargement of the Fed's homeroom, the Mortimer C. Eccles Building in Washington. "Though it's full of lovable characters it doesn't even touch on the origin and nature of money, and how it changed character through bank counterfeiting and government intervention. With the flag waving gloriously throughout its pages, it describes instead how the government-licensed banking cartel works, insisting that the monopoly we are forced to accept is for our own good."

She flipped through the pages. "There're lots of pictures in here, but there's one conspicuously missing. Can you guess what it is?"

She smiled and sauntered up to the camera. "I see some of you need a little refresher." She pulled her blouse loose from her jeans, lifting it enough to expose a tattoo on her lower left abdomen. As the camera zoomed in, the image on her skin came into focus as the Jolly Roger Dollar.

"This is what got us all talking about money in the first place. Why did the book hide from it?"

The video cut to a full view of Lisa with her shirt tucked in. She held the book up to the camera. "Wouldn't you know it? The answer's in the title: Monetary Theory for *Patriots* . . . Patriots being, in this case, those who obey and don't ask questions." She tosses the book off-camera.

"Okay, guys, coming soon to your favorite underground bookstore – that's right, another special issue of *Potomac Plowshare* presenting a different take on money and banking. It doesn't hide from anything. And it will give us the full meaning behind the Jolly Roger Dollar in plain English because it was written by the man who started this revolution, the former chairman of the pirates, Preston Mathews. And if you tell them Barbie Relic sent you they'll give you a 10 percent discount. Now let's see, 10 percent of zero is . . . well, you can figure it out. But if you forget your manners and don't mention Barbie they'll hit you for the full price. Any questions? See ya, guys, and don't forget your *Plowshares.*"

"Reminds me of a beer commercial," Gage said after viewing the video, which ended on a still of a winking Barbie. "Who on earth would take her seriously?"

"Beer commercials sell a lot of beer," Hawkins said.

Gage stared at the flirt on the screen. "And tell me again why this website is still in operation."

"We closed it but it came back again through a different ISP," Stewart said.

"A different ISP," Gage parroted.

"Don't worry, Chief," Hawkins added. "This is Barbie's swan song. She'll soon disappear into a black hole. Her and everything else on that lousy little website."

"An inflammatory tabloid publishing the work of the former Fed chairman," Gage mused, shaking his head, "and promoting it with a little tart and her tattoo. Christ, it's a rebellion on drugs. It would be hilarious if it weren't so pathetic."

Hawkins flipped the lid shut on the laptop. "Whatever. We've got it covered."

"Got what covered?" Stewart inquired.

"We've made arrangements to keep the poison off the streets. No one's going to be reading the Mathews issue of *Plowshare*."

"What!?"

"We've put a few junkies to work in exchange for early release. I have a feeling they'll be very reliable. They're being paid with seized crack. Quality stuff, Franklin tells me."

"You can't be serious," Stewart said. "That's unconscionable!"

"It's efficiency, Boy Scout. We're using the resources we have to protect the image of a leader . . . even if said leader attempted to change his image during the last moments of his life." Hawkins regarded him for a moment. "We're at war. Anything goes."

"Apparently the first thing to go is integrity," Stewart said. "Will these 'resources' be wearing armbands?"

Gage intervened. "Don't ask how sausage is made, Stewart."

Stewart was getting worked up. "Why are we worried about a tabloid piece, even if Mathews is the alleged author? Let him speak. *Plowshare* has the right to publish it. May the best ideas win."

Hawkins left the room in disgust. Gage sighed and made an attempt to muster some patience. "This isn't a high school debate club, Stewart. This is the real thing. Remember? We're here in the White House trying to run the damn country in a hostile world? Huh? Am I getting through? We're not at our lockers deciding what books to take home for homework. The wrong ideas can disrupt our . . . delicate balance, even if on some theoretical plane they're 'right.' Comprehend? We deal in reality, not theory, and the reality is Mathews' ideas could destroy us. So we destroy them first, okay? In any manner we can."

"If Mathews is just a kook he can't hurt us. If he's right, then I respectfully suggest, sir, he's trying to save us."

"We don't need saving, Stewart. That's the flaw in your logic. We here at the top are not in any danger. This world is about power, and it's never going to change. We maintain that power through education, police, and money. If any one of those three goes weak, our position is threatened. The Liberty Browser project will shore up the first of those three pillars. It strengthens the messages we can deliver, because they will not be publicly challenged. If we lose the battle of ideas we lose control. And without a central controlling agency we're sunk, elites and peons alike. Power therefore is not only good for us, it's good for the millions of morons who hobble through life bumbling from one job to the next, from one marriage to the next, without a clue. They wouldn't survive without us. Government is the engine of social order and harmony. And Mathews martyred himself to overthrow the government."

"I find that hard to accept. He ended his life as a goldbug. Since when—"

"—Not any goldbug. He was Preston Mathews, the former Fed chief, condemning to its very roots our system of money and credit."

"I hate to bring up ancient history, but didn't Greenspan do almost as much in his own weird way? We had gold before we had fiat money. And we had government back then."

"Compared to the size of government today, what we had then would fit on the head of a pin. And with a pinhead government society was being swallowed up by the powerful. It came down to a fight between the Morgans and Rockefellers. The money powers controlled everything. Fortunately, we had some intellectuals who put a halt to it with progressive social legislation. Government, in other words, needed to grow to stop the Robber Barons. And in growing it found itself incompatible with any semblance of a gold standard. Listen, Stewart – gold can't support the government we have now. Nothing can. We need debt, massive amounts of debt. Make no mistake, Mathews as a gold proponent is an enemy of the state. If we don't put a permanent end to his Jolly Roger crap, he'll bring us down and destroy the common man in our wake."

"Excuse me, Mr. President, but I must respectfully disagree with your history. It was the Morgans and Rockefellers, along with other big names, that pushed for more government-backed cartels and other interventions as a means of protecting their turf against competition. We've corralled the fox, but the fox is in charge of the corral."

"Well, whatever the facts are, great sage, big government is here, and we will perish without it. We need to protect our turf from competition, too."

Nina hung up the phone after a brief conversation with Suzanne Ward, who was almost positive the girl calling herself Barbie Relic is or was a Morrisville resident. Beyond that, though, she didn't know anything about her.

How in the world did a girl like that get involved with Preston's crusade, Nina wondered? If anything confirmed Preston's death, Barbie Relic did. No man of integrity would allow a tramp to promote his ideas.

Then again, the man she once loved for his integrity, left her. Nor did he take his integrity with him. He had become obsessed with admission into the power elite, and you don't get there by trumpeting sound money and honest banking. It could well be that the renegades carrying on his crusade see no problem trying to sell an honest gold standard like they would skin cream. It's certainly consistent with the flamboyant treatment he gave his barn. But even Madison Ave has a few rules. The BRC people have enough working against them already without resorting to a whore as a spokes—

Her phone rang again. It was Suzanne.

"I checked with my son, David," she said, "and he knows the girl. Her name is Lisa Beeman. She hasn't been back to school since the biplane drop."

"What does he know about her?"

"Not much. She was suspended from school twice. Once for violating the dress code, the other for swearing at a teacher. She has quite a rebellious streak – I guess so, if she dropped out of school. Maybe she sees Preston as a rebel like herself and feels inclined to help his cause."

"What a way to help a cause," Nina said.

"Nina . . . she's young and pretty. And she made some good points in the video. She acts loose, but it was meant in humor, and that's a popular style. She offered humor, youth, and beauty – and wisdom, if the *Plowshare* issue lives up to her claims. I'm not so sure she hurts his cause."

Nina sighed. "I don't know, Suzanne. I've talked myself into believing she's a blight. But maybe I'm wrong."

## 21

The Mathews *Plowshare* issue hit its niche sales locations only to be swept up by young adults who looked years beyond their age.  If their total intellectual capacity could be calculated it would exceed a random sampling of equal size from the general population.  But their intelligence lay dormant and corrupted.  They were specialists devoted to the arts of theft, deception, and denial for the purpose of acquiring a state-controlled substance on which they could get high.  Little else seemed to interest them, including responsibilities they might have incurred, such as children.  As long as it didn't involve work and the risks weren't prohibitive, they would do anything for a hit.  Swiping unread tabloids in exchange for little white rocks was easily one of those things – if such an offer were possible.

Thus, when the jails allowed people to see them who were not on their visitors list they became suspicious.  When they found themselves released early for good behavior as long as they agreed to commit theft for an unknown employer, an act for which they would be aptly compensated, they became paranoid. When they turned in bundles of unread *Plowshares* to a man in a white van for a key to a locker in a bus terminal, some were too scared to go, figuring that turning the key would trigger their dismemberment. But others were more daring, and when the keys opened doors to a decent payoff, they had good reason to use it, they believed, because no part of this deal made any sense.

Alexander, as was his policy, made the special issue available as a PDF download from *Plowshare's* website. Shortly after it appeared, however, his Apache web server came under a Denial of Service attack in the form of hostile pinging that resulted in a gross degradation of performance. What should have taken seconds to download on a high-speed connection was requiring hours. Consequently, the PDF remained on the server largely unread.

## 22

Ricky Sawyer sat in his cabin seven miles west of Suzanne Ward's split-level and watched a new browser install itself on one of his computers.  When the home page of the Liberty Browser opened, he glanced at the beta copy of the browser running on a machine to his left.  The beta had arrived on a CD several weeks earlier in a plain brown wrapper with a bogus return address.  After copying the beta to his computer, Sawyer sent an email consisting solely of the subject line *Thanks* to a friend who had a friend whose younger brother was a member of the Mag Seven.

For several seconds Sawyer's eyes shifted from one monitor to the other while he compared the two screens, looking for differences.  Both the beta and the official version featured a picture of the White House and various innocuous links, including "Fun stuff for kids" and "Traveling with the First Lady."

"Same face," he mumbled to himself, his voice rising on the last word. He exploded into a sneeze, then another. He sniffed and raised his immense weight, knocking over a cup of long-forgotten coffee, momentarily relieved it missed his keyboard, and moved with surprising lightness to a window across the room and slammed it shut. He sneezed again returning to his seat, a high-back with rollers on a plastic chair pad. Setting the pace for the rest of his décor, a carpenter's dust mask hung from the neck of a nearby two-liter Coke. He had tried the mask once but the sneezes kept coming, besides which it felt like slow death from suffocation.

After toweling up the coffee spill he dropped into his chair, sniffed, and typed a few words into the url address line of the official White House browser. He sniffed again. "Well, Liberty Browser, you gonna take me to Barbie Relic?" He hit the enter key. LB came back with the polite response, *Website currently unavailable.*

"Didn't think so. Let's try a few others." He keyed three more web addresses, each a well-known thorn in government's side, and Liberty Browser turned him away each time:

*Website currently unavailable.*

"Picky about who you let me visit, aren't ya? As Charles Bronson might've said, that fries my ice. But if you want to be picky . . ."

He rolled over to his left. The beta copy of Liberty Browser still showed the White House home page. He closed the application and launched a different one that ended on its own in less than a second. Then he re-launched the beta.

Liberty Browser beta came up with an altogether different look. He nodded. "Now let's see if it works with the real thing."

He took a deep breath and turned to the computer on his right, closed the official Liberty Browser, and ran the same quick application. Then he re-launched Liberty Browser. "Oh, man," he said, "what has the devil done?" The government's browser appeared the same on both monitors.

A lively passage from Mozart's *The Sleighride Dance* began playing from somewhere behind the monitor. He reached in back of it and nudged a box of microwave popcorn aside to get to his cell phone.

"Hey . . . Yeah, it just installed itself . . . You, too, huh? Well, you'll be pleased to know the horse ran fine in prime time. Do you want the modified version renamed? It would be a snap to do. . . Okay, I'll stay with LB. So tell me if this is still the plan: Barbie will have the monograph, and a little fairy dust will make LB a homebody . . . Yeah, two weeks sounds about right. LB should be the only browser in town by then . . . See ya."

He slid the phone behind the monitor and looked at his screen for a moment, absorbed in thought. He took a sip from his empty coffee mug. His breathing got thicker.

Sawyer was not afraid to take big risks, as he had proved by cracking the Fed's computers and showing Mathews the results. It was surprisingly easy to do, really, after he had been cleared to interview Mathews for a paper he was writing for his ex-wife's class. On the day of his visit Mathews talked to him briefly then passed him on to other Fed bigwigs, three out of five of whom were eventually interrupted by mission-critical matters, leaving Sawyer alone in their offices for mission-critical minutes of his own.

Only in a reluctantly-granted follow-up interview did Mathews get to see how Sawyer spent his solitary moments on his previous visit. Sawyer told him he hacked the Fed as a public service, to expose its frail security. If he had had malicious intentions he wouldn't be confessing it to the top man himself, he insisted.

Even if he revealed himself to be Snow White, Mathews told him, the government would show no mercy. He would be quietly arrested on vague charges but never go to trial. At some point before the trial, he would become the victim of an unfortunate accident. Or maybe the government's henchmen would simply do away with him before the arrest. In any case, the government was not about to show the country, especially Wall Street, how vulnerable it was by going public with the crime.

"I'm going to forget what you told me," Mathews told him after quiet deliberation, "provided you do, too. But I will expect the favor returned someday. Do we have a deal?"

"We have a deal," Sawyer said through the wad of cotton in his mouth.

"Breaking this deal would be very costly to one of us. Very costly. Perhaps that person is me. Or maybe it's you. Which do you think?"

Sawyer shook his head. "We have a deal," he repeated in a raspy voice.

"Good. But don't worry about the favor. It will require you to be loyal to principles, rather than an institution. If you

were looking to do something big with your life, you should be
very interested in what I have to offer. Enough said for now.
Lips sealed?"

"Sealed," Sawyer croaked.

*Don't worry about the favor. Don't worry about the favor.*

Right. He was about to step on the toes of a vindictive
giant. For what? For *principles*. What principles? For freedom
and sound money. Such things are in *our* self-interest but
damned sure not the giant's. Sawyer was using his hacking
skills to do the man in the street a favor, but the man wouldn't
save him from annihilation. He wouldn't even have the
decency to mourn at his funeral. All Mathews had done was
postpone Sawyer's execution.

He grabbed his phone and fumbled it to the floor. He
picked it up and somehow tapped in a number. The phone
ringing in his ear sounded as soothing as a jackhammer.
Breathing seemed to require conscious effort, and a thought
labeled "heart attack" was waving a red flag.

"Yes?" a man's voice answered.

Sawyer squeezed his eyes shut and murmured a few
words to himself, invoking a  mantra. " . . . To be, no matter
where, a man . . . to be, no matter where, a man."

"Excuse me?" the voice asked.

He opened his eyes and leaned back to look at the rafters
above him. A ceiling fan hung suspended over his head, and
he would swear it was about to fall.

*"My God, man, what will they do to us?!"*

## 23

Gradually, as downloads proliferated over a three-week period, Liberty Browser became the eyes through which many Americans viewed the World Wide Web. As President Gage had promised, the new browser saw no evil. Political purity had arrived in cyberspace. On the American version of the WWW, Preston Mathews was defined as the late Fed chairman and no more. He had been an outstanding public servant whose life was tragically cut short in a private plane accident. There was no trace of corrupted dollars, suicide missions, or money drops. The lunatic fringe that fostered such nonsense had been snipped off in the public interest.

It had been a fight for freedom – freedom for government versus freedom for those under it – with the victor proclaiming the other side had won.

With Winston Marlowe standing behind him off to the side, Gage was basking in a press conference in a White House briefing room. For once, his smile actually reflected his feelings. He was carefree, light, joke-cracking.

"I don't know the exact figures off the top of my head," he was saying to a reporter, "but I know the number of websites that weren't invited to the Big Dance is on the order of one in ten thousand." He flicked a quick glance at Marlowe as if to confirm the statistic, then turned to the audience again. "So we're not doing anything Draconian. Most sites made the cut, a small handful didn't. This is a far better percentage than we see in the sports world or private enterprise when selections are made."

Hands shot up amid calls of "Mr. President!" Gage picked one out.

"The government browser lets us access numerous sites dedicated to gold investing and promoting a gold standard, yet barbarous-relic.com is not one of them. Can you comment on that?"

"Barbarous-relic.com was dedicated to subversion and malicious slander. Gold was merely its cover."

"Are you saying barbarous-relic.com was non-factual or misleading?"

Gage had his hand raised, ready to pick someone else. "Yes, I am saying that." He pointed to a man standing on the far side of the room. "Yes."

"President Gage, some anti-war sites have been excluded from the browser's acceptance list. What criteria was used in determining whether to include them or not?"

"There's a fine line between responsible criticism and subversion. As you've noticed, I'm sure, you can still find plenty of sites calling for my head. A lot of heat goes with this job, and anyone who can't take it shouldn't apply. But there were sites, for example, that went beyond common decency, such as those showing the mutilated corpses of American soldiers after an ambush, and I don't think that furthers the cause of our nation in the least. Our military personnel are thousands of miles from home defending our freedom, and they need all the support we can give them. They don't need reminding that war has its dangers."

"But sir, don't the people back home need reminding? If war isn't portrayed accurately how will people understand what it is they're supposed to support?"

"I think every adult American realizes that war is sometimes a necessary evil. Even that great critic of government, Thomas Paine, conceded as much in his famous *Common Sense* pamphlet. I don't think our cause is furthered by showcasing hideous details. Certainly, the families of the fallen don't need it."

"One last question: Some people maintain defending our freedom thousands of miles from home makes no sense since there are no ostensible threats at that distance. How would you—"

"—That's a very narrow, parochial view that American statesmen abandoned long ago. We are not an ostrich with our head in the ground. We are not isolationists. We have a moral mandate to bring freedom and democracy to every land where it is missing. Furthermore, our freedom is threatened by their lack of it, because countries in which freedom is missing tend to be belligerent. That's why it is perfectly correct to say our soldiers are defending our freedom. In bringing freedom to oppressed peoples they are defending ours. I want to thank—"

"—Sir, excuse me, but do you think a policy of perpetual war and foreign intervention is compatible with freedom at home? As our civil liberties are necessarily eroded through war-time measures, some claim we're a threat to world freedom instead of a defender of it."

Gage managed a smile. "Only people who have given up on America consider that argument plausible. I certainly do not. As everyone knows, we're still the freest country on the planet, and we intend to stay that way.

"I want to thank you for your questions and add one final comment. We sometimes hear people say government doesn't deliver on its promises. Do me a favor. Next time you hear someone say that, ask them to log on to the internet. We promised the American people a respectable web experience, and with Liberty Browser, we have delivered. The Liberty Browser has cleaned up a segment of our social life in desperate need of attention and thereby has strengthened the freedom and morals of our nation. I expect that other countries will look at what we've accomplished with some admiration. Thank you."

Gage and Marlowe left the dais with the reporters on their feet, applauding.

## 24

Two days later Gage was reading aloud about spiders and other wonders of nature to a first grade class at Mark Twain Elementary in Buffalo, Missouri. A handmade sign behind him read *Knowledge is Freedom* in recognition of Gage's public commitment to taxpayer-funded, government-directed, government-mandated education.

Hawkins and Stewart stood in the back of the room along with two reporters and a photographer, and no less than 21 admin people and teachers lined the sides of the room hoping to be swept up in the aura of power and goodness the president of the United States brought in his wake – or at least get their picture taken with him. Buffalo had been selected because three students had invited him there, according to what Hawkins told the media. Realists knew that Gage had been neglecting the heartland too much and needed to show his face.

Gage seemed quite comfortable interacting with the kids. They were eager to tell him about spiders they saw around their houses or farms, and one little girl named Jessie accused her twin brother Bubba of bringing a big rubber spider to class just to scare her and the other girls. "What did you think about that?" he asked her, lamely. "Well," she said, "Bubba is sitting right over there, and guess what? He's afraid of snakes! I know, 'cause I brought one to class the next day." "So you got even." "Yes, I got even, only my snake was real." Gage and most of the other adults chuckled. The young woman with her eyes glued to the floor and the crimson hue to her cheeks was their teacher, Miss Shelby.

Gage went on to recite interesting facts about whales, dolphins, and bald eagles. He then added comments about how important it was to take care of the world we live in or else we won't have such interesting creatures anymore. He asked the kids what they were doing to make our world a better place to live in.

Jessie had her hand up right away. "Yes, Jessie?" Gage said. "What are you doing to help poor Mother Earth?"

"My name is Jessie James. My brother's name is Jesse James, too. Isn't that funny? But we call him Bubba."

"Well . . . how interesting. You and your brother are named for someone famous. Can you tell us—"

"I'm going to be like the real Jesse James someday. My brother won't. He's afraid of snakes. The real Jesse James wasn't afraid of anything."

"That's true, he wasn't. So tell us what you do to make the world around us better."

Hawkins had been following the presentation and marveling at how safe he felt allowing Gage to interact with an audience unscripted.  These kids loved the president and could only contradict him in the most charming of ways.  Someday the country's leader will be able to hold an unrehearsed conversation with an adult audience, he mused, thanks to educational devices like Liberty Browser.

"I don't know," Jessie was telling the president.

"Well, perhaps you help your parents grow your own vegetables.  Or you keep your windows open instead of running the air conditioner.  Do you do either of—"

"We play outside a lot."

"Well, that's good to hear.  You like the outdoors."

"Yeah.  My brother used to spend too much time on the computer."

"But now he plays outside with you?"

"Yeah."

"Do you play hide and seek or tag?  I used to play those games—"

"Our computer's broken so he has to play outside."

"Well, maybe it's better for you that it broke.  You're getting fresh air and—"

"You know, it's not really broken.  It just doesn't work right.  Isn't that funny?"

"What's wrong with it?"

"Nothing.  It just doesn't do anything."

"That sounds like a sick computer to me."

"Yeah, it's sick.  My dad thinks it's funny.  But you know, my dad likes the pretty girl with the tattoo.  He's going to get in trouble, I bet."

Hawkins and Stewart looked like two men who suddenly heard a ticking sound but couldn't locate the source.

A nervous Miss Shelby spoke up. "Brandon, doesn't your mom mow your lawn with a push mower that has no motor? Can you tell us why she does that?"

"She doesn't do that anymore," a mortified Brandon said.

"Oh? Why did she stop?"

"Her boyfriend brings his over." Brandon raised his hand. "I have to go."

As Brandon headed for the door another boy named Justin stood up and spoke directly to Gage. "We're building an outhouse! You can come see it when it's done! Do you have an outhouse? My stepdad said you should because you're our leader. Do you have one?"

*My dad thinks it's funny . . . My dad likes the pretty girl with the tattoo.*

Little Jessie's words played repeatedly in Hawkins' head on the flight back to Washington. Not even JD No. 7 would keep her quiet. It was hardly shocking her dad liked the tattooed whore, nor was it strange his daughter should mention it. Kids did those things, especially daughters. Every computer he had ever messed with did flaky things on occasion, so it wasn't surprising she would say it was sick. But why in the devil would her dad think it was funny? What's funny about a computer that wouldn't do anything? He tried to convince himself it was just a kid talking, but he couldn't quite relax with that. *Something doesn't compute.*

By his third JD the issue was moot. He had fallen asleep.

25

It was close to two in the morning when a broad-shouldered SS agent named Elston knocked on Gage's bedroom door and entered.  At Dr. Soo Hoo's insistence, Fann Li was administering a feather massage accompanied by the relaxing sounds of a flute – zither duet.  Gage was in a deep slumber when Elston shook him gently and was barely half-awake a minute later when he was sitting on the edge of the massage table squinting at the agent.

"Mr. Marlowe wishes to speak with you, sir," Elston said for the third time.

Gage barely had a voice.  "Marlowe?  Marlowe.  Oh, Jesus."  He slid off the table and let Li put a robe around him. He seemed confused.  He turned to Li.  "Don't go away."  Then to Elston: "Let him in."

"Sorry to disturb you, Chief," Marlowe said in a low voice as Gage led them to a small table on the other side of the room.

"Not as sorry as I am.  What's up?" Gage said.

Marlowe tried to cover his jitters. "I'll have to try one of those massages sometime. I've never seen you so relaxed."

"Marlowe, you're this close—" Gage held his thumb and forefinger about a quarter-inch apart and offered it for Marlowe's consideration.

"Sorry, Chief. I'm a little – I don't know. I thought it best to tell you now, though, since I was informed you were still awake. We've gotten a few reports – very few, maybe eight or nine – that Liberty Browser is experiencing some problems. It doesn't appear to be anything serious. Serious in the sense of being widespread. At the moment we believe it's related to old versions of the operating system that some users run. The simplest fix, most likely, would be to have them update their operating systems. I want to stress – and this is important – I want to stress it's not the operating system per se that's at fault. Most likely the users haven't applied all the patches they should have. But since the systems are outdated, it might be better to encourage them to move up to a newer release."

Gage turned his face away, irritated. "For Christ's sake, you're jabbering like a lunatic. You're saying Liberty Browser doesn't work on some older computers. Is that right?"

"Yes."

"And you thought you should interrupt my massage to tell me about it?"

"I realize it sounds trivial but keep in mind this is something you've promoted heavily as the epitome of government competence. This is your baby – and of course for that reason it's mine too. I didn't want one of your friends to send you a newspaper with a Liberty Browser article circled in heavy red."

"Is Liberty Browser okay?" Gage asked flatly.

"Except for some old machines that haven't been properly updated, Liberty Browser runs perfectly.  And we're looking into—"

"What's wrong with those cases?  Does it not work at all?"

"It appears to go into an infinite loop – uh, it freezes on the screen."

"But in all the rest, the ones that have the latest and greatest operating software, or whatever the hell you call it, we're smooth as silk.  Liberty Browser works as designed. Right?"

"Yes.  Absolutely."

"Tell me again without blinking."

"Yes, sir.  There's no doubt about it.  Liberty Browser runs as designed.  But you need to remember, even a perfect browser is not idiot-proof.  As we expected, we've heard reports that can only mean some people are unfit to use a computer."

"What reports?"

"Stupid stuff.  Not worth your attention."

"You've brought it to my attention.  Tell me."

"There are a couple of small-town Midwest newspapers that have received phone calls from locals saying Liberty Browser works but won't take them to the paper's website.  We haven't checked into it, but it sounds like classic operator error. The papers said their people could access their website with Liberty Browser just fine."

"Tomorrow you will tell the rest of the country about the need of some people to update their systems. Don't mention the idiots. Since the browser is perfect, it's the user's responsibility to make it run right. I don't want the White House in the computer business. Keep it light. Downplay the problems. Make it look like you're on top of things, which of course you are, right? In no sense is this a serious situation, though there're bastards who will try to twist it into something serious. Do you understand what to do?"

"Yes."

"Good. Good night."

Gage headed back to Fann Li as Marlowe turned and left the room. She pulled hot towels from a steamer and laid them on the table, then, with a warm smile, handed him a small glass of her homemade strawberry wine. He sipped the wine, savoring its taste and smooth texture, while she removed his robe, leaving him in pajama bottoms. She took his glass then patted the table. He hopped up and stretched out on the towels.

They had had a discussion once about their relationship and decided the least stressful arrangement would be platonic. He considered that one of his better agreements.

"Tension lives in many places," she reminded him. "I think you'll feel better after we put some heat on your back."

"The internet," Gage said, "is one big leak. But that damn browser will save us."

## 26

Marlowe's announcement the following day was carried to all corners of the country, but what many people heard was a government bigwig saying something about an update needed for their browser to work right.

They were not surprised, therefore, when a message arrived in their inboxes a few days later with the Liberty Browser logo centered at the top.  The message said users should double-click the attached file to upgrade their copy of Liberty Browser to acquire new security features.  It was sent on behalf of Winston Marlowe, Chairman of the President's Critical Infrastructure Protection Board, which again most people took to mean Marlowe himself authorized sending it.

When they ran the update, a message greeted them thusly:

> This patch program corrects an access restriction problem in the current release of Liberty Browser, and is therefore recommended for all users.  To proceed, click "OK."  To cancel, click "Cancel."

Users who clicked "OK" and applied the patch found their browser afterwards to be an altogether different animal.

Liberty Browser thenceforth opened to a new home page: Barbarous-relic.com. It not only opened there, it stayed there, not unlike a TV set that could only receive one channel. When users tried to go to a different site, whether by toolbar icon, favorites selection, or address bar entry, they ended up right where they started: Barbarous-relic.com. Any attempt to go elsewhere simply refreshed the screen.

Users could venture out to other sites only through links on BRC. The links were all affiliates promoting the Preston Mathews rebellion. There was no way for users to access the web's great search engines or anything else. For those who ran the update, barbarous-relic.com and its links became the world of the World Wide Web.

Frank James, the father of Jessie and Jesse, called the Buffalo, Missouri *Telegraph* and told them the new patch was the same one he had received earlier. It, too, had turned the government's vaunted browser into a BRC browser. "Hats off to the guy who did this," James told an editor over the phone, referring to the virus. "Serves the bastards right."

*Telegraph* editors knew about Frank James. Soon after Mathews' flight ended at the foot of his barn, James rented a billboard in town displaying a simple logo – dollar signs in four corners with a Jolly Roger in the middle. The town council officially condemned it for aiding and abetting sedition and threatened him with prosecution if he didn't have it removed within two business days.

James complied and had a new bill posted – a picture showing stacks of gold coins with the caption: No State shall make anything but gold and silver coin a tender in payment of debts. Article I, Section 10, U.S. Constitution.

Council members declined to comment on the replacement, but within a week of its appearance the billboard was vandalized beyond recognition.

No one knew exactly how many machines had been converted to BRC-only web browsing, but the usual experts declared the number had to be in the millions. Nor could the problem be corrected by reinstalling the original browser; the patch program left a virus that re-infected it. Opening up the web to competing browsers was not an option the Gage administration was willing to consider.

Thus, the barbarous relic underground had usurped Liberty Browser's throne. Some bloggers boasted of having one of their machines deliberately infected as a way of joining the rebellion.

The hijacked browser had an embedded countdown meter that began at 259,200 and decremented by one every second. The meter was captioned, "Time remaining until deliverance." While anticipating that fateful moment users had much to browse on barbarous-relic.com, including Mathews' monograph, a PDF of the *Plowshare* issue that Hawkins had hijacked and prevented from electronic distribution through a coordinated DoS attack. It didn't hurt that Barbie Relic was available to gaze upon, either.

Marlowe had the glum look of a man entering the executioner's chamber when he proffered Gage his resignation in the Oval Office, where the president and Hawkins were having a meeting. Marlowe excused himself for the interruption, placed the letter on Gage's desk without making eye contact, and started to leave.

"Stay," Hawkins told him. To Gage, he said, "If you accept this letter we'll be in real trouble. We have an opportunity here, gentlemen."

"And what opportunity is that?" Gage asked, his mood surprisingly mellow and patient. Hawkins was concerned that Gage's latest disposition was a precarious defense mechanism presaging something truly dark, and he had no desire to see what it was. He knew Marlowe had been on his way to resign and had waited until now to initiate damage control.

"Let's look at the facts," Hawkins began. "Winston Marlowe is a high government official dedicated to serving the public weal. In common with other public sector leaders, he has renounced his lust for power and profit for a life of compassionate service to his fellow Americans. Marlowe's motives, therefore, given his status as a government official, are beyond reproach."

"Excuse me," Gage said, "but when are you going to get to the facts?"

"These *are* the facts – not the facts of reality, but the truth about what people believe. In spite of all their cynicism, they still cling to the myth we're here representing their interests. They believe it because that's their only hope, and they can't face life without hope. This perception of theirs, as wildly off the mark as it is, is the key to our survival."

"You sounded like you believed what you were saying," Gage said. "You had me worried."

"Stick with me. Now, listen: We remind the public that Marlowe works to make their life better, not to stuff his pockets with money or inflate his swollen ego. Since they don't dare challenge this, we've covered our moral behinds. Now consider this: Any piece of software out there is subject to attack. It's usually the most popular titles that get hit, too – victims of a hacker big game hunt, you might say. To the warped minds of the hacker world, the government's browser presented an irresistible target, and it got hit. *It happens all the time. No one will blame us.* Oh, they will at first but we'll set them straight through the media, who will regurgitate what we give them: 'We were trying to do good for the people and got bushwhacked.' Are you getting the picture? Since we're not selfish profit-seekers, we'll become objects of sympathy. As in any virus attack, the users will be victims – but we'll be martyrs. And they'll love us for it. Winston Marlowe and his staff will humbly go about fixing the problem, as good public servants would. And people will direct their wrath to the unknown miscreants who messed up a noble government project. If anything, this attack will win the hearts of a lot of doubters."

Gage had been nodding, somewhat agreeing, somewhat as an anxiety control device. His head came to a stop. "We always need to win the battle of the words, don't we?" he said mostly to himself. "I see once again why I hired you. The man with X-ray vision." He cast a dark glance at Marlow and waited.

Marlowe had listened to Hawkins spiel like a man devoid of volition, awaiting either exoneration or execution with equal indifference. "Tom presents a strong case for continuing the battle. I'm willing to go on if you're willing to keep me."

Gage tapped his fingers on his desk once. "How soon can you fix the damn thing?"

"We have contractors working on an antivirus as we speak. I'm anticipating something within the next 24 to 36 hours. As we've learned, when the meter hits zero access will be unrestricted, as before. At that point users can access our website and apply the fix. The big question is, will they? The media should step in and encourage people to do so, to protect their data as well as to avoid another hijacking. We might want to get Danny Flynn back and show him running the antivirus. We should run a series of TV ads showing different celebrities eagerly running the update. I think that would convince them. I would expect that in a couple of weeks most of the machines infected will be back to normal. Uh, Liberty Browser normal, with the restrictions in place."

"How wonderful," Gage said.

Later that day Mel Stewart presented the spin to the media, though in his case he really meant what he was saying. It didn't sell.

"They need to abandon their monopoly," Terry Parks told Vicki Prentiss's TV audience. "With so much commerce dependent on the internet, and so many people blocked from accessing it, the U.S. economy will take a big hit. Can we prevent it? Yes, of course, by opening up the web to other browsers. But other browsers allow access to sites we're not supposed to see. Power must be preserved at all costs."

But Parks wasn't quite on target. Many machines were not infected, including the ones at the Fed and on Wall Street. And as the countdown meters across the country touched zero, the World Wide Web opened up again. Liberty Browser would take users anywhere they wanted, including BRC.

In spite of a massive ad campaign, most people had no wish to return to the original Liberty Browser that enforced restricted access.

## 27

Nina fetched the 1893 keepsake gold coin from her purse and set it on Alexander's desk. "Take a good shot of it and post it on your website. Underneath, mention that you've contracted with a third party to write the forward to his book. That's all – no name."

"And you think that will bring him to the surface?"

"If he remembers anything at all about our marriage and what it once meant, he'll recognize this coin . . . assuming he's still alive. If he is, he might wish to get in touch with me again, given his recent turnabout. But then, this movement or whatever it is has a lot of craziness to it, so I really don't know what to expect."

Alexander had called her to ask if she was interested in writing a forward to Mathews' treatise, which he was about to publish as a real book with a quality binding and an index. Since the Liberty Browser hijacking, he had been inundated with emails asking for a bound version of the monograph.

Alexander laughed. "Why bother with tricks? I could just post a note on my website asking him to call me." He straightened up suddenly. "Hey, why not? I mean, why the hell not?"

"No reason. I'm sure you'll enjoy the avalanche of prank calls."

"Oops," he said. "Oops. Oops." He settled back in his chair. "So when can you get it to me – the forward?"

The question surprised her. "It should be in your inbox. As soon as you called I began working on it and finished in one sitting. I can't even sign my name in one sitting. If it's all wrong tell me and I'll try again. It may be too personal."

"Oh, lady! Around here the more personal the better. Wooden prose and tabloids don't mix. I can't wait to read it."

"Well, I also wrote it on the assumption he was gone. I don't know why – I really think he's out there somewhere. I said he should've been writing something like this at an earlier age, when honest money was the center of his professional life and one of the ties that bound us as a couple. But I thanked him for writing it now, as an apostate, even if it was the last thing he wrote."

"Did I hear you right? You two had feelings for each other *because of your views on money?*"

"In the tradition of Pierre and Marie Curie, so I hear . . . we began as partners taking on a great enemy together. We devoted our lives to the issue of honest money and how it became corrupted and how it leads people down the path to debt, slavery, and war. 'Partners' doesn't describe it – more like 'trench-mates'. Trench-mates who became spouses." She looked down for a moment to steady herself. "Then ex-spouses. And finally . . . what do you call a divorced woman whose former husband has martyred himself?"

"Heartbroken, if she still loves him."

She forced a smile and nodded. "I suppose that's true. Though I really don't know."

"First you rode a rocket together, then you were cranked through a wringer. Money is more than a political issue to you."

"It was first and foremost a personal issue. When someone devalues wealth I have earned then blames it on someone else, I take that very personally."

"And how did you feel when you knew he was the one doing the devaluing?"

"It was the first time in my life I felt compelled to reject the testimony of my senses. I cannot get past the impossibility of it. I can't. I've never been able to believe he was really the Fed chairman. When I think of that I start thinking of aliens in space ships and brain control experiments. It's more believable that way."

"So you don't hate him?"

She thought for a moment. "I don't know what I feel. I'm damn curious to know exactly what happened to him. But beyond that . . ."

"And most people consider inflation a boring topic."

"It *is* boring – if you turn to the standard accounts. But the boredom serves an important purpose." She slapped the side of her face in a gesture of mock-scolding. "Conspiracy talk. Bad girl."

Alexander leaned forward. "I hate boredom," he said. "Can't stand it. *Can't stand it.* If I couldn't do this – whatever *this* is – I'd be a gangster before taking an honest job. Even though we do a lot of mundane things here, they're done for an exciting purpose. Or at least *we* think so."

"But you are a gangster," Nina said with a hint of a smile, "though maybe not literally."

"That's exactly right," he said. "I am. If it weren't for Mathews I'd be state enemy number one. Right now their best strategy is to ignore me. Someday they'll decide to get rough with me. To them it'll be like swatting a fly."

"You really believe that? You think they'll just come after you?"

"Sure. Why bother with the nuisance and publicity of legal action?" He slapped his desk top. "Get it over quickly."

She frowned. "You're martyrs."

"Not quite, sweetheart. I leave that to people like your ex, if he's not around anymore."

"What do you mean?"

"I have a contingency plan."

Alexander had his staff produce an index to go along with Nina's lead-in and got into the mail order book business. He placed an ad on his website that included a picture of Nina's gold coin, and response was overwhelming. Within 24 hours of the ad's appearance he received 391 orders for a book whose contents were available free on barbarous-relic.com. His Apache server, armed with improved tomahawks, suffered no ping or other attacks.

One of the orders came from Terry Parks, who reviewed it in great detail five days later in the *Times*. He ended his review by saying he was gift-ordering copies for President Gage and Fed Chairman Wallace. He kept his word, even paying for overnight shipping and gift wrap.

Alexander received no phone calls about the gold coin in his book ad.

A well-known investor authored an article for the *Journal* that praised Mathews' book for explaining the business cycle as the necessary consequence of fiat note issues and bank credit expansion. "An honest international gold standard," he concluded, "would remove politics from money and create a stable investment environment. Central banks would go the way of dinosaurs, and the world would be far more peaceful and humane – not to mention prosperous." Several other financial writers began to cautiously praise Mathews and gold, saying that "perhaps it's time to revisit the idea of gold as money."

Most financial commentators followed the government's cue and ignored Mathews and his book. A few cultural critics avoided the economics of money and limited their remarks to the "cruel, stingy world" a gold standard would impose. "The beauty of government-controlled fiat money," pop psychologist and Harvard Ph.D. Peter Allport wrote, "is how it puts ownership of the nation's wealth under control of the people we elect, albeit only indirectly. Otherwise, when people are allowed to keep the money they earn they have a tendency to hoard it. Such self-centered behavior has no place in a compassionate social democracy. A return to gold would

condemn the world's impoverished millions to death from
starvation and neglect.  If fiat money is in fact an authorization
to inflate, it is a small price to pay for saving humanity from
the stony indifference of the barbarous relic."

## 28

It looked pretty much like all the other small farms she'd seen. The only things missing were the owner and the big red barn.

The wind tossed her hair and carried a scent of burnt wood, even now, months after the plane crash and fire. She was standing near the place where he had rendered a silent battle cry. The FBI's crime scene tape was gone, as was the FBI; the only evidence they had been there were signs posted around the property bearing their familiar greeting:

FBI warning:
No trespassing under penalty of fine and imprisonment.

She had parked behind the boarded-up house. The neighbors could see her if they tried hard enough. There was no reason for them to try.

She could visualize him standing here painting the barn. He would be on a ladder or perhaps a scaffold detailing his artwork. He had a plan. Did it include martyring himself? That part didn't fit the person she knew, but then the person she knew had changed. Idiotically, she found herself looking at the ground for footprints or some other sign he had left the crash unscathed.

She looked again at the open space of earth where the barn had made a defiant last stand. Unlike other barns that go away this one wasn't destroyed by accident or a random act of nature. Designated men had taken it away, out of public view . . as other men took away the Mathews *Plowshare* issue. Preston had known from the beginning what they would do, which is why he took pictures . . . which is why he sent the letter to Suzanne Ward . . . why he wrote the monograph.

The question is, *when* did he write them?

And if he's still around where was he? How could such a familiar face stay hidden this long?

*They've confirmed zilch so far*, Terry Parks had said. He was talking about the pilot. But if the pilot left the plane before it crashed, when did he do it? He would be flying way too low for a parachute to save him. And how did he direct the plane to impact where it did, so that it would light up the painting without torching it? Maybe a great stunt pilot could pull it off, but Preston? The Chairman of the Board of Governors?

She turned and began walking, following in reverse what she thought had to be the flight of the plane as it journeyed to earth for the last time. Was there some clue out there waiting to tell her how he escaped death? Ahead of her was a gravel pathway of sorts skirting the perimeter of grassland that was once cultivated corn field.  The pathway ended in tall grass and other plant life, but she plowed ahead, wading her way through thick growth.  Other than her plodding footsteps the only sounds she heard were the singing and calls of distant birds.

She stopped and turned to look at the missing barn once again, now perhaps seventy yards distant.  That barren, scorched plot of earth was the blood of a massacre.  Yet, what appeared to end there was in truth a subtly worked-out beginning.  An anachronistic little plane had cruised over the spot where she was standing and started a fire that lit up the country's grass roots.  The edifice removed by the FBI became the fallen flag-bearer of a revolution.

She continued her trek and caught a leg on a tall weed that sunk its thorns through her pants and pierced her skin.  She unraveled herself from her captor and moved ahead toward a thicket and a stand of trees, behind which was a little pond.  As she worked her way through the scrub to get closer to the water, the full size of the pond came into better view.

On the other side of the water was more of the same brush.  She wondered if his property included Preston Pond or if she was gazing at some other owner's little lake.  And if it was his, for what had he used it?  To jump in from a biplane?  He wouldn't have the guts, besides which it was too shallow.  He'd break his legs and drown.  Then why the pond?  He didn't buy the farm to farm it.  He—

—*bought the farm.*

But he didn't buy the farm, damn it! He had no reason to. Surely he would know BRC would make the government sweat. Why would he want to miss that?

She was making too much of this. She looked up. At this point in his flight he would be – what? – a hundred feet or so in the air. That's as good a guess as any. A hundred feet up and moving. He sets up bales of hay – no, not bales, not enough give to them – a haystack, a humongous haystack, too big to miss. He's probably drugged a little anyway if he had already flown into a thunderstorm over Morrisville, so he gathers up his nerve and jumps out. A few seconds of freefall terror and he's in the belly of the hay, too scared to spit but otherwise intact. The plane hits, the revolution begins. He slips away and goes into hiding.

Great. So, where was the hay now? Did the wind scatter his haystack? Every bit of it? How convenient.

Well, it didn't have to be hay. What about one of those nets trapeze artists sometimes put under them? She looked around. He could set it up almost anywhere. He could stretch it between trees and make a monster hammock. And the fact that the net's missing means he hit the mark. He lived to take it down. Preston, the circus daredevil!

Sure he was.

A jingle played from somewhere in her pants. She pulled her cell phone out. It was Suzanne.

"Hey," the caller greeted. "Did you go?"

"I'm here," Nina said, "standing by Preston Pond with the birds, mosquitoes, and bullfrogs. And God knows what else."

"Preston Pond?"

"A pond hidden behind what was once his corn fields.  Oh, my God!"  A barn owl had left a tree on the opposite bank, swooped low to the water, and was headed straight for her.  She ducked and squealed as it passed over her head.  It landed three-quarters up a nearby tree.  "What's with that bird?!"

"What is it?"

"An owl.  It just – an owl!  There was an owl in the picture Parks took after the plane crash."

"They're good to have around.  There's one in the woods behind us David would like to make friends with."

"Tell him he can have this one.  It came right at me!"

"Are you sure it was you and not something else nearby?  Have you checked your hair recently?"

Suddenly panicked, Nina swatted an imagined owl hors d'oeuvre from her head and scooted to a different spot.  "No, there's nothing on me," she said, trying to sound calm.  "I think."

"Then I guess he just likes you.  Some owls like humans."

"I think it's time for me to leave."

"Call me when you get home."

"Bye."

"Bye."

Nina slipped her cell phone into her pants pocket, turned, and saw the white scarf.

It was half-sunk along the edge of the pond and entangled with various weeds and other muck, and only after moving closer was she sure it was a scarf and not a piece of white litter.  She carefully rescued it from its captors and stretched it out by the ends.

She felt numb. This was almost certainly the scarf he was wearing when he posed with the Barbarous Relic before final takeoff. Shouldn't it have been obliterated, along with the rest of him? Or did it just happen to break loose over this pond?

"You found his scarf," a deep voice behind her announced.

Nina yelped and whirled around. Some ten feet away, an old man was looking at her with a half-smile, wearing long Navy blue jogging pants and a matching jogger's jacket.

"Sorry. Didn't mean to scare ya."

"Who are you?" she managed.

"Nobody. Live up the road a ways. But I knew Dr. Mathews. Nice fella. Saw your Jeep and thought I'd see where you were."

"Well, I was just leaving."

"You're his wife – his former one."

"How did you know?"

"Saw you on TV years back, doing an interview. Couldn't understand why you two would break up, but that's another story. Guess you want to know if he's still around. Lot of people do."

"You know where he might be?"

"Nope. Haven't the slightest idea. But I do – I do know somethin'."

"I see." She guessed him to be near 80, with sparkly blue eyes. He was lean, slightly taller than her, and gray hairs poked out from the sides of his head, giving him a slightly crazed look. The jogging attire, replete with quality running shoes and a digital watch, was the finishing touch.

"Yep. Did a job for the doctor not long ago that I thought was strange at the time. Not so strange now, though."

"What job was that?"

He moved closer, until he was arm's length away. "I can keep a secret, can you? Most people can't. He didn't swear me to secrecy, exactly. Just asked me to keep quiet about it. Y'know, finger to pursed lips. He paid me in cash. Paid me a lot more than I would've asked. Is that called hush money?" He chuckled, apparently amused at the hint of conspiracy. "I don't know. If I had known what he was up to I would've done it for nothin'. I haven't mentioned it to anyone. Figure you have a right to know, though – if you can keep a secret. Never known a woman who could."

"Loose tongues are part of the package, I'm afraid."

"Darned if I don't agree."

"And in my case I've got two counts against me: I'm also his ex-wife. You know about them, I'm sure."

"If the wrong ears picked it up . . . But I could make an exception in your case. You're not typical. If you were typical you wouldn't be back this far. You wouldn't be here at all. Mind you, if word reaches the government, I'll play dumb. They'll believe it. I'm old. Don't let this outfit I'm wearin' fool you."

"Then I guess you're covered. What's the deal?"

He cleared his throat. "Well, this," he said, nodding at the water behind her. "This pond here. Five months before he went down it was no more'n a puddle." He smiled. "Not anymore. I took care of it for him."

Later that evening, per her usual routine, Suzanne sat with David and Denise as they did their homework. Nina showed up with a small bottle of California Merlot just as the kids were going to bed. A half-hour later the two women began drinking and didn't stop until the bottle rang hollow. They tried to picture a Fed chairman leaping from a diving biplane into a small pond that had been excavated by an old and possibly unstable neighbor. It was suggested by one of them – neither was sure who the next morning – that Nina had fallen for a geezer's little joke, that the old fool planted the scarf and made up the story about deepening the pond. This was assigned a low probability, however, even if he *was* wearing runner's garb befitting a man forty years his junior. As the last drops of wine disappeared, they were in agreement that Preston was either stuck in the mud at the bottom of the pond, reincarnated as a barn owl, or still alive somewhere.

At Suzanne's insistence, Nina spent the night on the couch. Sleep was out of the question, however, even with the help of the wine. As Nina stared alone into the darkness, emotions and memories converged and took their toll. As much as it hurt, she was still unable to cry.

Had Nina driven home that evening she might have shared the highway with Ricky Sawyer, who was headed east to meet two men at a Dunkin' Donuts in Arlington. Two local police officers ate at the counter while Sawyer and his buddies huddled over coffee at a booth. Plans were made calling for bold action. The fight was to be taken to the enemy, and that, in spite of the risks, was a great relief to all three.

188 THE FLIGHT OF THE BARBAROUS RELIC

**29**

Mainstream pundits started attacking Mathews not for what he stood for but for what they considered his political backstabbing.  He had deliberately suppressed his real views on money, they charged, to reach the position of Fed chairman.  He then used the great eminence of his position to smear the central bank as a coterie of counterfeiters.

"One can hardly resist comparing him to other revolutionary lowlifes who mastered the arts of ruthlessness and propaganda to lead their countries to ruin," one nationally syndicated wit spouted.  "For if we let this dissembler take us to his promised land, we will find bank runs and panics the order of the day, with common folk losing the savings of many years because of a mere crisis of confidence in their local bank."

But Mathews' following continued to grow, especially among knowledgeable commentators who troubled themselves to read his monograph and its bibliographical references.  As they pointed out in their commentaries, it wasn't gold that brought on the runs and panics, but the banks' longstanding practice of fractional reserve banking. Gold, of course, took the blame and fractional reserve banking – the scheme by which banks create new money from nothing – continued on without fear of market retribution, thanks to the government-backed central banking cartel.  As one of them explained: "True, we have no bank runs today, but neither are today's banks storing sound money.  The value of our fiat dollar will decline whether it's kept in a bank or withdrawn from a bank and kept under one's bed."

Investors began calling the White House demanding to know how they planned to deal with the Preston Mathews phenomenon.  They had built multi-billion dollar strategies based on the fiat dollar's orgy of debt, and this was no time to go honest on them.  They wanted the Mathews crowd silenced or answered convincingly.

Doug Foster took most of the calls that came to the White House.  It was strange seeing him handle irate callers from major investment houses, but he succeeded on the premise that their most urgent need was hand-holding.  That and some political tough talk he had learned from Hawkins.

Hawkins, in fact, happened to be in Foster's office when Foster took a call from a man named Emmett, whose firm was currently No. 2 in the league tables, as they were called, a highly-disputed ranking system applied to investment banks based on the value of their deals.  Foster had had lunch with Emmett less than a month earlier and found him pleasant company.  But there was something in the way he screeched "Foster!" on the other end of the line that suggested today's call would be an entirely different experience. "I'm in conference with the president's Chief of Staff at the moment," Foster told him, "but let's talk."

"No, *you* talk!" Emmett shot back. "We're in a boat that left shore a long time ago, and I want to know where it's taking us. Don't push me off on Wallace because he's hiding behind his desk. And don't tell me it's his decision. Everything in D.C. answers to the White House sooner or later. This is no time to change the rules of the game. We've got our asses sticking out, all the way out, and we're counting on you guys to cover us. *And you can't cover us with gold! You can't, Foster! We can't go that way again! Not ever! We've set our tables! This is the way it is! We underpin the whole goddamn economy! You can't get academic on us now!*"

Emmett didn't need handholding. He needed CPR. "I can tell you the following with absolute certainty," Foster said. "As an active and growing government we have every incentive to protect our fundamental methods of operation. Radicals are boat-rockers and we have no use for them – especially when it comes to money. Money is your blood and ours; Wall Street doesn't exist without it, government doesn't exist without it. So you might say our interest in this matter is more than vested.

"As long as this government exists, we will control the money supply. We will control what passes for money. We regard people who interfere in these matters as enemy combatants. You're well aware of how we deal with tax rebels and private counterfeiters. We regard the Mathews following as far worse. They're trying to take money out of our hands and put it in the hands of the free market. We've been trying to get rid of the free market since the Great Depression, and we're almost there. Are you listening? We are not – I repeat, we are *not* – going to reverse our policy.

"Every sane scholar, no matter what his or her field, has rightfully condemned the free market as a Hobbesian nightmare, the great enemy of prosperity and social justice. As evidence, look at the Mathews Rebellion. They're trying to put us, the people's representatives – and, quite frankly, their saviors – out of business through monetary deprivation. They're trying to undo over a century of beneficent government growth, a period in which, by sheer coincidence, smart investors such as yourself have amassed great fortunes. The Mathews rebels are terrorists. They are mortal enemy number one. We don't reason with mortal enemies. We eliminate them."

After a pause he added, with a self-satisfied glance at Hawkins: "Do you have any questions so far?"

Hawkins had watched and listened in utter fascination. He shook his head and left, wondering if Foster would show the same calm nerve if his caller was confronting him in person.

30

Investors and government's corporate "partners" continued to be served in such fashion but lesser mortals of the work world were raising doubts on the web or through afternoon TV talk shows that called for a new offensive. Hawkins figured that turning Foster loose on everyday folks would not go over well, so with Gage's approval he decided to step up personally and put the matter to rest on the show second in popularity only to the World Wide Web itself, the Vicki Prentiss Nightly Journal on Eagle News.

Hawkins, wishing to avoid the perception of being on a level with a media type by sitting next to Vicki in the studio,· arranged to appear through a remote feed into his polished office at the White House. He gave her a list of questions to ask, the answers to which he rehearsed in advance. She balked briefly but went along. Vicki's superiors had spoken with her at length about her Browns show and some of the questions she had raised. They let her know they were unhappy with her speculations and that as popular as she was they could always find "another smile and pair of legs" to replace her. Vicki resigned immediately. After three heated phone conversations with her agent, who acted as mediator, apologies were made all around and her status was restored.

Hawkins also arranged to have the intellectual support of Dr. Peter Allport through a remote feed to a studio in Arlington, where he was currently hopping about promoting his latest book, *Accepting What We Must.* Vicki was to get Allport to slip in some comments about the moral necessity of accepting a liquid currency if we are to meet our obligations to society's underclass.

On the night of the show, which Eagle had heavily promoted, Vicki looked as perky and beautiful as ever – from a distance. In her usual style, she sat on a tall padded stool with a notebook and pen, wearing a blue blazer and white skirt that exposed shapely legs. She kept a pitcher of water and a glass on a tall table next to her. As the camera moved in and brought her up-close, however, discerning viewers would notice her eyes had lost some of their sparkle, that the energy she projected was more mechanical than natural.

After some welcoming remarks she commented on the legacy the late Fed Chairman Mathews had left, or appeared to leave, with the cult of gold lovers. Was the former chairman involved in a movement that undercut his function at the federal reserve or were certain people exploiting his death to promote their agenda?

"For help with this question and related issues, I've invited the president's number one man, Thomas Hawkins, to our show tonight," she said.

TV viewers saw Hawkins sitting behind his desk in a dark suit wearing a confident smile.

"Good evening, Tom."

"Hello, Vicki. Thank you for having me."

"What can you tell us about this Preston Mathews movement that might clear up some misconceptions?"

"The first thing I do is thank the Lord he didn't leave a family behind. They would be seeing a good man's reputation ruined on the basis of some offhand comments he once made about gold. This kind of thing happens often, unfortunately. John Maynard Keynes, the last century's greatest economist, is repeatedly criticized on the basis of his obiter dicta rather than the cogent mathematical proofs his critics are unable to comprehend. Something similar is happening to Mathews."

"Tom, some people have speculated that Chairman Mathews survived the plane crash on his farm and is directing the gold movement underground."

"Vicki, I'd like your viewers to see this official FBI photo taken at the scene of the crash." A picture of the flaming ruins of Mathews' biplane appeared briefly on screen. "It ain't pretty, but it was reproduced in newspapers around the country as well as on many websites. How anyone could believe a human being could survive a crash like that surpasses rational understanding. Dr. Mathews' life ended tragically in this accident. Rumors to the contrary are total fabrications."

"Some people claim he bailed out before the plane crashed."

"Those people are mistaken. His remains were found in the plane. Besides, his plane crashed at a low angle to the ground. It would be impossible to parachute from a plane flying that low. Nor did he jump from the plane onto a large marshmallow before it crashed. The truth is, unfortunately, that Preston Mathews died in the manner supported by the crash site evidence."

"Barbarous-relic.com had pictures that were quite disturbing," she said. "One showed Chairman Mathews standing beside his golden biplane next to the words 'Barbarous Relic' wearing a proud smile. And the more infamous one showed a barn, reputed to be his, painted with a likeness of the American dollar, with the symbol of piracy replacing the first president's portrait."

"I think most Americans agree with me that that image is an obscenity. This Mathews movement is the product of slick con artists who are devoid of any sense of decency. To replace the father of our country with a pirate flag is a vicious affront to our traditions. And to impute the authorship of that deranged dollar to the Chairman of the Board of Governors is a hateful offense to the memory of a good man. As for the scrawled message on his biplane, I can't believe any American truly accepts that at face value. With the computer technology available today, a child of nine could doctor a photograph with that inscription in a matter of minutes.

"We can judge the caliber of this movement by the saucy young girl they have selling his alleged book on the web," Hawkins continued. "Where'd they get her, MTV? Flaunting her body tattoo of the demented dollar to the camera – it's an obvious ploy to distract viewers rather than encourage them to think about the meaning of the symbol. It's the lowest form of marketing. No man of Mathews' reputation would ever be associated with such a tactic.

"I want the American people to understand – Preston Mathews died in a tragic plane crash and has no connection whatsoever to the Jolly Roger dollar or any of the other nonsense being perpetrated on the internet."

The camera cut back to Vicki. "In trying to understand what might motivate someone to construct such elaborate fabrications, we've asked bestselling author and psychologist Dr. Peter Allport to share his views." Vicki smiled at an off-camera monitor. "Dr. Allport, welcome to the—" Her smile suddenly vanished, and she blinked twice rapidly.

The man filling the viewer's screen was decidedly not Dr. Allport.

"Excuse me, Vicki, but doc saw a ghost and ran for his life," the surprise replacement said. "Perhaps I can help you, though."

The camera cut back to Vicki. She was on her feet steadying herself with the stool, her notebook and pen lying on the floor.

"Jesus Christ! You're alive!"

The viewers' screen went wacky, as if the technical crew running the show didn't know who to put on camera. In the space of a few seconds the screen flashed from Mathews, to Vicki, to Hawkins, and back to Mathews again.

"Keep the camera here for a moment, if you will," Mathews said. "I'm Preston Mathews, the former Fed chairman, and I'm very much alive. I want to tell your viewers, Vicki, that I crashed my plane to draw attention to the criminal organization I once led. The Federal Reserve's system of money and credit is – by design – nothing more than a sophisticated counterfeiting operation. Folks, the Fed is robbing you blind and causing a great deal of economic and moral havoc. It exists to serve special interests, and most likely that doesn't include you. If the human race is to have a future, we will abolish the Fed and liberate money and banking from government control. If we let the market work I believe it will choose a gold coin standard with full reserve banking, as many economists recommend and which I discuss in my book."

Mathews paused for a moment and smiled at the monitor. "Vicki? Any questions?"

The camera switched back to Vicki. *"Questions?! Questions?!"*

"Let me help you out," Mathews said. "Is my pirate dollar obscene, as Thomas Hawkins states? By substituting the pirate sign for Washington's face, all I've done is unmask the fiat dollar for what it is: a hoax and a means of steady plunder. Where's the obscenity? Exposing the fraud with an appropriate symbol or deceiving people with the face of the father of our country?

"I also want to say that Barbie Relic, our spokesperson for the sound money movement, has done an outstanding job and at present has no connection with MTV, though that could always change. She wants to spend her professional life in front of a camera, and unlike Mr. Hawkins, I believe most people don't object at all to seeing her on screen."

When the camera cut back to Vicki, the sound had been cut off, but not the entertainment. Two older men in dress shirts and ties were trying to pull her off the set, while she thrashed her arms wildly and otherwise put up a good fight. She made a final lunge to break free and threw one of them on his backside.

The station broke for a marathon string of commercials.

## 31

Stewart and Gage had been watching the show in the annex to the Oval Office. They had been sitting when the show began. They were now standing, and Gage abruptly bolted for the door leading to his office. His sudden departure startled Stewart almost as much as seeing Mathews' ghost. He had expected perhaps a head-splitter requiring pills and Fann Li or a trip to Hawkins' office to do some shouting. But why Gage would want to charge into his own office choking on his spleen left him bewildered.

Then the explosion came – a string of threats and obscenities. He heard a desk drawer slam shut. Stewart rushed into the world's most famous office and saw the president of the United States headed out of it, his right hand clutching the handle of a 9 mm Glock 19.

Gage moved surprisingly well, but Stewart tackled him to the floor as Gage came to a stop in front of Hawkins' desk and was raising the gun at him. Tech support for the telecast had mercifully vacated the area. The former Scarlet Knight lineman tucked the fumbled handgun under his belt behind him, hoisted Gage up and left him there while he lunged across the desk with both hands and dragged Hawkins over the top of it, knocking precious memorabilia and an antique brass table lamp onto the carpet. He grabbed both men by their shirt collars and marched them into Hawkins' private conference room, slamming the door shut with his foot. He pulled the gun out from his belt in back and tossed it on the floor. The whole scene had overtones of an outraged principal disciplining delinquents who had crossed him once too often.

But he wasn't through. With looks of utter disbelief on their faces, he drove them back against a wall, knocking over a chair and almost losing his balance. He screamed into the president's face: "What are you, some holdover from the Third Reich?! Have you lost your mind?! Were you honest-to-God going to shoot this bastard? I'm tired of you sons of bitches running this country like a banana republic!" He released them and stepped back, fighting for self-control and struggling for breath. "We're going to deal with this situation in a responsible manner or surrender the ship to some other bunch of fools. Got it?!"

Gage was crimson. "What the hell do you think— "

"—Shut up, or I'll put you both out of your misery right now! Your jobs are to lead the country – lead it without ditching the principles on which it was founded! You've got a huge responsibility! Quit screwing up!"

"You're crazy," Gage said, and meant it.

"Damn right I'm crazy! Crazy enough to call a press conference to announce your resignation. Don't want that? Then think! Work within the law!"

Stewart's chest labored for air, his eyes had taken on a predator's piercing gaze, beads of sweat stippled his forehead. There was no trace of his former loyal self. Gage and Hawkins seemed to regard him as they might a snarling Doberman – dangerous at close range but of no significance otherwise.

"The law can't catch him," Hawkins said. "What do you suggest we do?"

The question seemed to surprise Stewart – he blinked several times. "Okay. For starters, instead of sending a hit squad after him, invite him here for a meeting."

Hawkins could scarcely conceal his contempt. "Yeah? And discuss what? How to switch back to a system of gold and abolish the Fed? We might as well nuke the whole country. It'd be more merciful."

"I don't know the answers. I only know that honesty works, and that we haven't tried it in a long time. If you guys have better ideas than Mathews, then debate him in a civilized manner. Invite him in here and talk it out!"

"Best ideas win, 'ey, Stewart?" Gage needled. "Just like in high school. Or was that fixed too, and you didn't know it? Did your school get tax dollars? Probably. Then I'll guarantee it was fixed. We're not going to fund our own destruction. Who the hell would do that? Your precious, pristine high school debates were fixed. Our election debates are fixed. Everything is fixed by men you don't see. The men who fund the government make sure it's fixed to their benefit. It's a law of nature. Locke was wrong. Natural rights are a myth, useful

202 THE FLIGHT OF THE BARBAROUS RELIC

only for political purposes. That's why you don't hear about natural rights anymore – they're no longer useful. In the end there's only one truth, and that's what we say it is because we have the money and the power to back it up. Neither Mathews nor God in heaven can change that. But he's trying to, and we're not going to let that happen."

"So all this talk about us being a democracy or a republic is pure bunk," Stewart said. "What we have now is a fascist police state coming into its prime."

"What we have *now*," Hawkins said, "is democracy in a more mature form. The natural leaders have taken over. Big surprise. If you want to assign an ugly name to it, go ahead."

"Ever consider just leaving them alone?" Stewart said abruptly. "The people – just leave them the hell alone. Let them live their lives." The blank expressions of the other two told him they hadn't, that such a notion was beyond the range of decent discourse. "So the plan is – what? Sic the goons after him? Hold another Vicki Prentiss special and wait for him to show his face again?"

Hawkins exchanged a quick glance with Gage. "Actually, no," Hawkins said. "We don't really have a plan yet – how could we, for Christ's sake? – but I believe it will end up looking very much like what you wanted. Mathews will come here, and we will have a talk. But we won't have to invite him. He'll come on his own, I'm quite confident."

"How are you going to manage that?"

"By putting some heat on his friends."

"What friends?"

"For one, that lousy little tabloid that's publishing his book."

"What about them?"

"We need to shut them down and arrest the owner."

"On what charge?"

Hawkins shrugged. "He's a business. Take your pick. It's an open-and-shut case. He's guilty on more counts than I could name."

"That's dirty," Stewart said.

"It's the law."

"And what if Mathews doesn't take the bait?"

"Well, aside from seeing his publisher face criminal charges—"

"—We'll deal with that if it happens," Gage interrupted. He straightened up, seeming to remember he was supposed to be in charge. "We're wasting time. This is a goddamn lousy situation. We've got to get moving."

"We'll get Franklin going on *Plowshare* right away," Hawkins said. "First thing in the morning."

Gage turned a lethal eye to his Chief of Staff. "'Come again?"

"I'll call him right now. I may go with them."

"I can't imagine it happening any other way." Gage brushed past Stewart and walked out of the room.

Hawkins stared at the gun on the floor in disbelief. "Son of a bitch," he blurted out.

32

When Suzanne called, Nina was correcting papers at her kitchen table with a red robe hanging loosely over the pajamas she had on.  Her right foot was tucked comfortably under her left leg, and a mug of green tea sat soothingly nearby next to her portable phone.  Without taking her eyes off the paper she was reading, she reached for the phone and brought it to her face.

"Hello?"

"*He's alive!  Nina, he's alive!*"

"Who's alive?"

"*Who do you think?!  You're not watching TV?!*"

Nina sat up suddenly, her foot slipping to the floor.  "Oh, my God!"

"He crashed Vicki's show tonight and kicked that twerpy Harvard collectivist out of his spot!  And what he said!  He pulled the rug out from under Gage's top jackass!  It was pandemonium!  It was wonderful!  He's *alive*, Nina!"

"I'm completely overwhelmed."

"Do you think he'll call?! I think he will! I'm surprised he hasn't called already!"

"I don't know. I—maybe. I can't think."

"Call me when he does! Bye!"

Nina had to set the phone down with two hands. She was shaking. *He crashed her show and usurped one of her guests? Jesus Christ. JESUS CHRIST!* She should turn the TV on and get the details. She didn't want to. Let him tell her directly.

She stacked the papers neatly and stood up. Having decided she would be useless for the foreseeable future, she moved to the couch and sat with her feet nestled under her and the phone cradled in her lap.

*He's alive! He's alive!*

She called Suzanne back. "I wasn't dreaming, was I? You really called?"

*"Yes!!"*

She continued sitting and waiting. As the minutes passed she thought of the ups and downs of their time together. She wondered what his first words would be when he called. Would he be light, serious, a little of both? She tried to imagine. And what would he do next? Would he stay in hiding or – or what? Maybe he would want to see her.

She was too excited to think.

She drifted in and out of sleep as random thoughts came and went, as the minutes accumulated into hours. She felt like a teenager waiting for her dreamboat to call and ask her to the big dance.

No one called.

She had fallen asleep again, and when her eyes opened the clock over the TV said 4:22. She was exhausted. And wired. She wondered what he was doing at that moment. Was he having a sleepless night? Where was he?

And with those questions a different door opened. And the view it afforded was not at all pleasant.

She had been a damn fool.

If he wanted to call he would have. But he didn't, and he won't. And it's not like he didn't have a reason to call. She wrote the intro to his book. She got Alexander to post a picture of the gold coin on his website. She's been an unwavering advocate of the ideas he's trying to sell. It's not possible he doesn't know these things. At the very least he could've called to express his appreciation. But he's obviously too busy for that kind of thing. He's probably too busy right now. Wherever he is, no doubt that little tattooed tart is right by his side – if not closer. A young thing like that would fall all over herself for someone like him, and obviously – *obviously* – he's more than willing to let her.

And here she sits waiting like an idiot– *an idiot*!

She stood up and paced. Was there a creature alive more pathetically naïve than her? No. Of course not. Whatever she might have learned during her studious life, it most definitely didn't include an understanding of men. In that respect, she was still a child.

Never, she told herself . . . never again would she allow this to happen.

## 33

It was convenient for the forces of government justice that Alexander housed his operations in a part of town where no one would call attention to the arrival of three covered troop trucks and a Jeep. Each truck carried 10 heavily armed, invincibly armored agents, most of whom loved the smell of blood as long as it was someone else's. Hawkins rode with Franklin in the Jeep and had told him he could bring in as many agents as he thought necessary for a quick mop-up. According to Franklin's intelligence, Alexander had six employees, none of whom had criminal records or prior experience with firearms, so he figured five agents per woman would do the job. The agents could share in the responsibility of getting the renegade ringleader.

Franklin's intelligence also told him about Alexander's office having only one door. Agents would have to climb steps, make a 90-degree turn and rush into the chambers single-file, exposing them to unknown hazards. It was not the most advantageous situation, but since they were arriving at

8:30, only a half-hour after the *Plowshare's* office opened, Franklin thought he could catch the women half-awake.

Leading the troops into battle would be 6'-6" John "Wayne" Wynne, a muscular African-American whose brain was connected to Franklin's by radio. "Wayne" and his troops each carried M4 carbines having a firing rate of roughly 800 rounds per minute, though their magazines were limited to 30 rounds each. This was not their normal crime-stopper, but given the political nature of their mission Franklin was taking no chances. At headquarters one of his lieutenants had suggested using Less Than Lethal firepower based on the known characteristics of the perps, but Franklin rejected it outright, saying, "It was shock and awe time."

The trucks and Jeep pulled into the *Plowshare's* weathered parking lot and stopped some forty yards from the entrance. Signaled by a double-blink of the Jeep's headlights, Wayne descended from the back of his truck. His troops quickly followed in silent obedience, pouring out of the other vehicles and falling in line behind him. With their elaborate protective gear they looked like an intergalactic landing party. Crouching slightly, Wayne led them across the parking lot, up the steps to the door and stopped.

"They move like a giant bug with a hundred legs," Hawkins remarked. He and Franklin were gazing at the long assemblage. "If I thought they were human, I'd actually feel sorry for them," Hawkins said.

Franklin turned to him, miffed. "The agents?"

"The riff-raff inside. Let's get it over with."

Franklin moved the small radio to his mouth. "Director to Special Agent."

"Special Agent Wynne awaiting orders, sir," Wayne replied. Through his face mask he glared at the sign above the door: *All the dirt they'd rather we not print.*

"Let's roll," Franklin commanded.

With push-button response, Wayne yanked the door open and led the charge inside.

It was a battle they would not soon forget.

Not only was the enemy missing, so were the enemy's weapons – computers, books, pictures of friends and family, and the countless other minutia that comprise an office. The only evidence of neglect were the overhead lights. They were still on.

Wayne and his men tried to draw the enemy out by shouting threats and firing randomly into the walls, but no one gave themselves up. They found a door leading into a large storage area with skylights, but even that was mostly empty.

They had attacked a vacant building.

Wayne radioed Franklin with his findings. Hawkins overheard. "Stewart," he muttered with dark vindictiveness. To Franklin he said, "Let's go."

When they arrived at the entrance, Franklin paused to order removal of the *Plowshare's* "dirt" sign while Hawkins went inside.

Secure in the belief he was unopposed, Hawkins strutted about with an air of bold fearlessness. "The damn cowards," he said to no one in particular. "How brave they look behind their traitorous screeds. But when someone finally stands up to them they beat it back to their holes. . . . This place makes me sick." He turned to Wayne. "Get rid of it – all of it."

Hawkins and Franklin hit the floor and shielded their heads with their arms, while Wayne and three other agents opened fire and turned the place to rubble. The noise was excruciating. When the shooting was over Wayne pulled his head gear off and gazed at the devastation. "There's a lesson here somewhere," he said to the room at large. With a huge smile he turned to Franklin, who was getting to his feet along with Hawkins. "The rebels got some cleaning up to do, Chief."

"I'd say so," Franklin said, straightening himself up. "Good job, men. Let's—" He froze. "What the hell's that?"

A jaunty little tune had begun playing nearby. It played slowly, as if someone were cranking a jack-in-the-box so as to savor every note. When Hawkins recognized the melody as "Pop! Goes the Weasel" he felt his testicles shrivel. "Where the hell's that coming from?!" he screamed. "Is that someone's cell?!"

No one bothered answering him. In the next instant they were all cursing and rushing to the door. The attempted escape produced a struggling pileup of helmets, chest protectors, assault weapons, and a couple of suits. As the men shoved and cursed one another, the toddler's tune continued its inexorable march to the grand finale like the cold hand of death.

But the big pop arrived unnoticed. The screams of trained killers unable to exit a warehouse overwhelmed all other sounds.

When the anticipated explosion failed to materialize, Wayne pulled himself free from the pack and began to investigate. Hawkins followed him. In a corner of what had been Alexander's office, amidst mutilated office debris, a smiling toy clown was bouncing on a spring from an opening in the floor. A note was pinned to its hat saying, "Hi, Little Boy." Alexander had rigged a harmless child's gadget to go off in his office.

Hawkins cursed and grabbed Wayne's M4. When he tried to fire at the clown nothing happened. "What's wrong with this goddamn thing!??" Wayne reached over and flicked the safety off, but Hawkins was too enraged to notice. He began beating the clown with the butt end of the M4, lacing the air with heartfelt obscenities.

To arrive at two plus two equals four one must know, among other things, the meaning of the terms on either side of the plus sign. As they were leaving Silver Spring Hawkins was fully knowledgeable about term number one, the jack-in-the-box clown with the "Little Boy" note – both words capitalized – but it took a radio chat with Wayne a half-hour later to put term number two in place: that the lights were on when the troops arrived. Even still, Hawkins did not see them as components of an equation until some time later when he realized both terms had been deliberate acts. When the number four emerged as an answer to a question he only now thought to ask, he looked frantically at his watch; they could never get back to the *Plowshare* in time. It was then that the impact of the morning's events took on a weight he could not bear. He started whistling, something he never did. He had no idea what he was whistling and neither did Franklin, who found it annoying.

Finally he stopped. "Ever been in a guerilla war?" Hawkins posed to the FBI man in the Jeep's back seat.

"I've never been in any war. Why?"

"Either have I. But I think we're getting a lesson in guerilla warfare today."

"Are you talking about the clown?"

"That's part of it."

Franklin laughed. "I hardly think a stupid prank—"

"Here's a prediction. I could be wrong. I hope to God I am. There's always a chance a stray bullet might have saved us. But if not, I predict you, me, your man Wayne, and the others will soon hit prime time." Then his voice rose an octave, as if he were delivering the punch line of a terribly funny joke while trying to keep a straight face. "You and I will get top billing."

"What the hell are you talking about?"

That Franklin didn't get it was too much. Hawkins broke into laughter. He laughed for a good half-minute, his eyes glistening with tears. Then he settled.

"Our downfall, actually," he said with dark amusement.

But it was a downfall with distinction. The video that swept the internet, showing the events from the break-in to Hawkins' clown assault – all shots taken from somewhere in the ceiling – was silent except for a track of music. Accompanying the soundless caper of the office invasion was a soulful jazz-trio performance of "Send in the Clowns," its plaintive melody suggesting viewers were witnessing a tragedy far beyond the futility playing before their eyes.

## 34

Nina could neither bring herself to teach exclusively the monetary gospel according to Mullins nor turn in her resignation. She decided she would wait for the enemy to kill her – teach as she always had until department head Keefe came by and literally showed her the door.

She wondered whether the stunt pulled on Vicki's show would give the board new-found courage. She was quite certain they would show astonishing bravery if they were guaranteed the rebellion would come out a winner. But with the world's most powerful government trying to crush the movement, she concluded her dismissal would, if anything, come even sooner.

And for that, she knew who to thank.

On the day following Hawkins' *Plowshare* invasion, Nina was in class discussing the 1848 House of Lords case, *Foley v. Hill and Others*. The case presented the English government's – and subsequently the American government's – position regarding the ownership of funds deposited in a bank. She read aloud a portion of Lord Cottenham's fateful decision:

> . . . money placed in the custody of a banker is, to all intents and purposes, the money of the banker, to do with it as he pleases; he is guilty of no breach of trust in employing it; he is not answerable to the principal if he puts it into jeopardy, if he engages in a hazardous speculation; he is not bound to keep it or deal with it as the property of his principal; but he is, of course, answerable for the mount, because he has contracted . . .

"So what does this mean?" she asked the class. "It means the bank can do anything it wants with their depositors' money and not be held criminally liable. As Rothbard puts it in *The Mystery of Banking*, 'if the banker cannot meet his contractual obligation he is only a legitimate insolvent instead of an embezzler.'

"In the days when gold was money, if you left gold coins on deposit at a bank, the teller would give you banknotes that read, 'payable on demand in gold coin.'

"Would you not assume the bank was safeguarding your deposit?

"Would you leave your gold on deposit if you knew the bank would use it to engage in 'hazardous speculation'?

"Would you leave it on deposit if you knew the bank was going to issue more notes than it had gold on hand?

"How else could it meet its obligation to pay on demand unless all its notes and deposits were backed by gold 100 percent at all times?

"And if it did issue fraudulent notes – notes not fully backed by gold coin – would it not be guilty of 'a breach of trust'? What do you think?"

As hands shot up, the door swung open just far enough for Keefe's matronly assistant to poke her head in the room.

"You've got visitors," she said, her voice unsteady. "Out here."

"Now? Who?" Nina asked, wondering why the normally chipper woman looked like she had had a frightful scare.

At the White House Gage had performed the miracle of getting Hawkins and Stewart to meet with him in the Oval Office. Any one of the three was more than willing to kill the other two, yet they were seated and dressed in the traditional garb of the American political class, holding a conversation in elegantly appointed surroundings. Hawkins had accused Stewart of tipping off Alexander, which Stewart hotly denied. Gage decided to accept his denial. He also decided to accept Stewart's apology for the rough treatment the previous night because of the patriotic motivation behind it. Hawkins refused to accept it – even though Stewart had likely saved his life – but agreed to work with him to get the Mathews case put away for good.

"Alexander has been in politics a long time," Gage said. "We shouldn't be surprised he anticipated an invasion. He's

Mathews' publisher. That alone told him he was targeted."
He paused for a moment of hate. "The bastards!"

He rubbed the sides of his head and continued. "But I
have a plan. A new plan. And it will work. I really believe it
can't miss because it's so very simple. I got Foster to research
Dr. Stefanelli's class schedule. A couple of Secret Service
agents were waiting for her outside her classroom today. She
should be here within the hour."

Gage's words hit Hawkins like a punch in the gut.
"Who's—" he began. "You're bringing in Mathews' ex?"

"She will be our guest here for awhile. Most men would
toss their ex-wives an anchor if they saw them drowning.
Mathews, I think, is a different sort. If he thinks she's in
danger, he'll cooperate. He'll know she wouldn't come here on
her own, so he'll know she's . . . well, you get the idea. I'm
going to ask her to issue a public plea for him to stop the stunts
and discuss his grievances like a responsible adult instead of a
college prankster. If he doesn't cooperate, his support will go
in the sewer. I expect him to make himself available here, for a
talk."

"What if she refuses?" Stewart asked.

"We'll make it very clear that cooperation is in her best
interests." Gage leaned forward. "Stefanelli will issue a plea,
and Mathews will come calling."

"Mathews might not go for it," Hawkins said. "He knows
we can't keep her here for long."

"Not normally. But she and I will make special
arrangements. She will agree to accept my invitation to stay
here until Mathews joins her. It's really very simple."

Stewart was quietly seething. "And what happens when Mathews stops in for a chat?"

Gage shrugged. "Then we've got him. We'll have both of them. And we'll make new plans. We're halfway there already."

"What plans?" Stewart pressed.

Gage smiled. "Mathews will make an apology. A public repudiation. A declaration that someone forged his book and pressured him into denouncing the Fed. Something along those lines. Now look – I'm going to address the nation tonight about all this stuff. I'm going to conduct it as a press conference. A press conference among friends. Stefanelli will make a brief plea at the beginning and step down. She is to be kept confined to her room before and after her appearance. Is that clear?"

Hawkins stood up. "Jesus Christ! You're putting her in front of the country?! On prime time TV?! Why didn't you—" He choked off his sentence.

"Why didn't I consult with you first, Hawk? Is that what you were going to say? Oh, I don't know – I suppose I went with a gut feeling. Yes, she could say something stupid, but that wouldn't surprise anyone at this stage, would it? And on the subject of stupidity, Foster showed me the internet video of yesterday's visit at *Plowshare*. Believe it or not, 'advice' wasn't the first word that came to mind when I saw it. I'd say we have some work to do, don't you agree? I think the lady from John Taylor U. will help us out."

"You're panicking!" Hawkins burst out. "This is the most half-assed, half-baked—"

"—If you'll excuse me," Gage said in a threatening tone. "I have a talk to prepare."

35

Ben Levy cut his swim short that noon hour and returned
to his office feeling just as agitated as when he left to go
exercise. He told his secretary not to bother ordering lunch
and to cancel a senior staff meeting scheduled later that
afternoon. And he meant cancel, not reschedule, when she
asked about it. He managed to wrap his reply with a pleasant
smile, then wondered if that would cover his condition or
further reveal it. Then, without understanding why, he called
Mel Stewart and arranged to meet him at a little park near the
Pentagon.

Although he didn't know Stewart well he had always felt a
kinship with him. Perhaps it was their athletic background
that created the bond or the suspicion that they shared a sense
of decency that found no outlet in their line of work. It
certainly wasn't their tallness, he knew. At 6'4" Stewart had
him beat by a good eight inches.

"In case you're wondering, I don't have a job to offer you," Levy said as they shook hands and began a desultory stroll among a scattering of sightseers and office workers.

"That's a relief," Stewart said. "Unless it was something away from all this. Far away."

"You, too? I'm not surprised."

"When I was a little kid I wanted to be a fireman. I still do, in a way. Imagine if you could clean this city up with a powerful hose. Go into a joint session of Congress and knock them all out of their seats with a blast of water. Can you see them scurrying out of the building into the sunlight, their pricey garments torn and dripping wet, and screaming about some madman disrupting the smooth running of government? Maybe they'd take the hint, do you think? But I wouldn't start with Congress. I'd pick a certain building on Pennsylvania Avenue. I can see the footage on the evening news – the pack's top dog tumbling and sputtering twenty feet above ground on a jet of water."

Levy grunted. "You'd have a lot of people helping you man the hose. But I can also see lawyers lining up to sue you and every one of your relations five generations forward on more counts than you thought possible."

"If the lawyers lined up in one spot—" Stewart mimed gunning them with a big hose. Then he shook his head. "God, I can't believe I'm talking like this."

A soft-rubber flying disc suddenly skidded on the ground in front of them. It was an iridescent green with the initials "P.S.N." marked on it. Stewart picked it up and snapped it back to the youngsters who were playing with it. "Thank you!" a blond-haired boy of about three called out in a Southern accent. Stewart gave him a little wave and smiled.

"That's what really gets to me," he said, watching with surprise as the little guy flung the disc with authority to his playmates. "Kids like that and how they're brought up believing we're a nation of laws protecting their freedom, and how the people in government are all honorable except for a few bad apples. I feel like knocking some heads."

Levy turned and spat. "All this muck we see – a good system would clean itself up, flush out all the garbage. But a good system would have good people. Ours has degenerated to the point where we each act as gatekeepers to make sure good people are marginalized. No offense. In a very subtle way each of us passes through a security checkpoint first, to make sure we won't ruin it for everyone else. But through the wonders of language we cover it up in our public statements."

Levy halted and stuck a hand out to stop Stewart. "How did he do it, Stewart? How the hell did he get Gage to nominate him? How the hell did he get past the Senate hearings. I haven't heard anyone in the media raise these questions. I don't understand it."

"He was a big mouth in the economics community," Stewart said. "He knew when to say yes and when to say no, and who to say it to."

"Don't get me wrong," Levy said as they continued walking, "I really don't like Mathews much. He's made me confront my own rot. I could've gone on living a happily ignorant life if it wasn't for him. It's not easy for a man to admit he's a coward, especially a military man like myself. But that's what I've been – a coward. That's just the damn truth. It hit home when that Morrisville woman read his letter. I tried every lousy trick I knew to get her to cave. But she stood her ground. And her townsfolk disowned her for it. She was the hero, I was the bastard. She was ostracized, I was an object of sympathy."

"Don't feel like you're alone. It's not like there are saints waiting to take our jobs."

"Y'know, I chose a military career because I thought like a child. I wanted to help defend the freedom bequeathed us by our Founders. Can you believe it? I haven't defended anyone's freedom at any time in my life. Not ever! All I've done is help put down resistance – in some cases, the resistance of people fighting for their right to scratch out an honest living. I was told there were strategic reasons why they couldn't exist but some thug of a dictator could. That's why I took the offer to move into Treasury. I thought there I could do some good. Collecting taxes is fundamental democracy, right? Who could dispute that? We may not like it, but it's necessary." He spat again. "Hell, it's just the pipeline that feeds the racket. Get the people to believe robbery is patriotic, then automate it. Tell them withholding is for their convenience. They bought it, and now most of them don't even think about it anymore. It's the most beautiful racket ever devised. Except possibly for the one Mathews headed up."

"The weird thing is I agree with you," Stewart said. "And I'm officially an advisor to the president . . . I played ball in college. I had a strong work ethic and did well for myself. You thought like a child? Beat this – I thought my positive role model would help clean up politics. Seriously, I did. But I never played ball against the kind of people I found in this place. I've been a glorified pawn, a useful idiot."

"In government, we're all useful idiots, to one person or another," Levy said. "When you centralize idiocy, as we've done, everyone suffers. That was the beauty of federalism – minimize the scope of idiocy. Mathews wants to go beyond federalism. He wants to divorce government completely from money and banking. He's the people's only hope, and most of them don't know it. Have you seen the *Plowshare* raid video yet?"

"Don't have the stomach."

"I lost mine watching it. I thought, these are the guys I'm shaking down the average Joe to support? When I saw a creep like Hawkins pounding a toy clown for squashing his ego I knew I was working for the wrong outfit. I don't know what I'll do, but I can't go on like this."

They walked for awhile, then Levy added: "And I'm not just talking. I mean it. I feel like setting fire to my office. Too bad he doesn't have tanks in his rebellion. He might could use me."

Stewart stopped walking. He looked at Levy and started to grin. "Not tanks. Something more subtle – Mr. Secretary."

"You've got an idea."

"Yeah. I think so."

## 36

Doug Foster whisked by staffers without greeting them or making eye contact and went into the small room in the corner of the West Wing.

"Hello," he said to the unsmiling woman seated on the couch, closing the door behind him. He approached her briskly, with a hint of a smile. "Dr. Stefanelli, I'm Doug Foster."

She raised a limp hand, and he gave it something akin to a handshake. He took a seat in a chair across from her.

"I apologize for the lack of cordiality in our manner today but we're especially pressed for time. You have been brought here to make a statement during the president's press conference tonight, and here is what you will say."

"Go to hell."

He tried to smile, but ended up wincing. "I understand. Really, I do." He handed her a page printed from a computer. She took it but let it lie in her hand unread. "As you can see – or will see – it is brief. You needn't memorize it, just familiarize yourself with it. In fact, you're encouraged to rehearse it. There will be a teleprompter in front of you on the dais. This is what you will say, and this is all you will say. You will not ask for questions nor take any that might be offered. You will not ad lib. When you finish, step down from the dais. A Secret Service agent will escort you to your room. Do you have any questions?"

"I'm a prisoner here, is that right?"

"My goodness, no. The White House doesn't have prisoners. You are a guest and will be accorded every consideration."

"So I can leave anytime I wish?"

"Certainly. Provided you have the necessary approval."

"And you really expect me to read a government-prepared statement as if it were my own?"

"Yes, I do."

"Do you plan to shoot me if I voice my own thoughts?"

"I think you're a smart lady and will know better."

She took a moment to read the statement. "The president really wants to meet with my ex and me?"

"Yes."

"That's not going to work."

"That's not your concern. You're only responsibility is to read the text."

"But someone wrote the text believing it was the right thing to say. I'm telling you it isn't, whether you consider it my concern or not."

Foster hesitated. "What part do you find objectionable?"

"For one thing, what's in it for Preston Mathews?  So far, he's running a pretty good revolt.  Why should he risk meeting with the enemy?"

"Because the enemy has his wife."

"The enemy has his ex-wife.  And believe me, the emphasis is decidedly on the 'ex'.  I don't particularly care what happens to him.  And I can guarantee he feels the same about me."

"All you're doing is asking for a meeting, not a tryst.  You don't have to like each other."

"Explain to me how I would keep the contempt out of my voice."

"You'll do fine."  Foster stood up.  "Just read the text."

"Look, your people have been watching me.  They know my phone calls, mail, email, class schedule, spending habits, everything.  They know there hasn't been any contact between us since way before his Halloween flight.  And the contact we had then was quite acrimonious, as I'm sure they also know.  Someone on your staff has made a serious blunder, and it could cost him his job.  I know failure is generally rewarded in government, but not in a case like this.  If this goes south, I really think heads will roll."

"Why are you, of all people, so suddenly concerned about government's fortune?"

"Because it's a waste of time, and I'd like to go home."

"Just—"

"—I know, just read the text.  Don't be surprised if I substitute a recipe for sauerkraut."

Foster gave her a dirty look and left in a huff.

"So you want to know if you've really got a Mathews' ally," Wallace said to Foster over the phone. "I'd say the odds are pretty good."

"Because of the Senate committee transcript?" Foster said.

"Right. It's not proof, by any means, but given what he's done since then I'd say he never abandoned his gold position. Certainly his former wife hasn't."

"So even though they divorced, you think they could unite to fight a common enemy."

"The divorce is the wild card. They're obviously in close agreement now on money and banking issues, but that doesn't mean they like each other. If the divorce was ugly, he could hate her enough to let her rot. And unless you knew them closely, I don't think you could determine how bad it was. Even if it was hateful, though, time tends to mellow the emotions. So, I think you're playing pretty good odds, even if they still carry some unkind feelings. I could see them helping one another without a bond of friendship or anything closer."

"I've never been comfortable with odds, not when the stakes are high."

"Look at it this way: even if he's an apostate on money, the fact that he's returned to gold in such high style would make it more likely she would forgive him. But if he duped the Senate Banking Committee during the nomination hearings, and if she knows he did, then they could be very strong allies, in spite of the divorce. Conclusion: I don't think he'll ignore her."

"Thanks, Mr. Chairman. I needed the reassurance."

"We'll all know soon enough, won't we?"

37

Stewart knew two fundamentals about Fann Li beyond what pleased the eye: One, she was the favorite assuager of the Chief Executive's response to crisis, and two, she dreamed of having her own TV show. Though Li's time with Gage would certainly help her reach that goal, at some point she would have to show the world and any potential TV producer she was comfortable in front of a camera. Why not show them now? Stewart reasoned.

Li's office at the White House looked more like a tiny health food/ spa retail outlet. There was no mahogany desk, just racks of vitamin and mineral products, a massage table, one floor mat, and a fancy stationary bike. When Stewart arrived at her place a little before seven, she was toweling off from a long stint on the go-nowhere bicycle.

"Hi, Fanny," he said while walking in.

She smiled. "He need a fix?"

"Actually . . . he does need a fix, but not the usual one. This is kind of short notice, but he needs a big favor."

"Whatever I can do."

"The lady who was to appear briefly on his press conference this evening has taken seriously ill, and we've made arrangements to take her to the hospital. It so happens she was to read a statement from the teleprompter that could be read by anyone, with a couple of minor changes." He smiled, hesitating.

"And . . . you want *me* to read it? On TV?"

"You would be performing a great service if you could. And think of the publicity you would get for your own show business aspirations. Given your background at the White House, showing your face on TV like this would all but clinch an offer."

Li blinked nervously. "Well . . . that's – wow! And all I have to do is read something?"

"Six sentences, to be exact. A plea for Preston Mathews to work with the president in resolving his differences rather than continue to put the country through unnecessary hardship and anguish. You'd be through in less than a minute, but you'd be on the air long enough for the right people to see how you handled yourself."

"I'm his masseuse. Who cares what I think about Preston Mathews?"

"Oh, only a few million people, I would guess. People who could more readily identify with you than with Mathews' ex-wife. You're someone working on a dream. Most people have dreams, too. If they saw that you cared about this issue, they might feel the same way."

"And Mr. Gage has approved?"

Stewart hated what he was doing and wished he could trust her enough to tell her the truth. "No. Not yet, at least. I've decided it best not to tell him about Mathews' wife taking sick while he still has time to worry about it. I'll wait until the last moment, then say I asked you to do the reading as a favor to him. I'm confident he'll approve. But if I'm wrong all he can do is kill the idea. He certainly wouldn't think any less of you. In fact, if he saw you were willing to help him out, it could only be good for you."

Li blinked some more and looked around. "I work in the shadows. I haven't spoken in public in a long time. What if I messed up?"

"The only 'public' present will be a few dozen media people and TV crew. You won't be facing a big crowd. Fanny . . . fear is the greatest killer of dreams. Don't let it happen to yours."

She took a deep breath. She managed a smile and a nod.

And Stewart left, managing not to loath himself too much.

"She's what?!" Doug Foster exclaimed.

"Vomiting. Dr. Hoo will take care of her. It's just anxiety. No worse than the migraines Gage gets and treated the same way." Stewart had stopped Foster in the decadent surroundings of the West Wing.

"I want to see for myself." He started to walk off.

"Go ahead, if you want to make her worse. You got her sick in the first place."

Foster stopped. "She certainly didn't fall apart when I talked to her."

Stewart waved his hands in exasperation. "Maybe she had a delayed reaction! How the devil would I know? All I'm telling you is she's sick. I think it's a reaction to the statement you're making her read. She'll be fine if you just leave her alone."

"And what if she isn't fine?"

"Listen, pal – she'll either recover or she won't. The show goes on either way, right? Our best bet now is to let her rest."

"Yeah, well, you're going to tell Gage, not me."

"Don't worry. But I'm going to wait a bit. The less time he has to foam about it the better. We don't need two people on stage suffering from nerves."

Foster's eyes narrowed. "Just for your information, Stewart, any treatment she gets will be here. All the limo drivers are on notice not to let her leave."

"I know. I told them myself."

## 38

A white Mercedes pulled up to the North Portico entrance of the White House where Mel Stewart stood waiting with three house maids. A light rain was falling. The driver of the Mercedes climbed out and opened the rear door. The maids climbed in back, Stewart in front. The driver closed the door, returned to the driver's seat and pulled away. It was, to all appearances, an uneventful happening.

After the Mercedes passed through the gate onto Pennsylvania Avenue, the driver looked in his rear view mirror at the maid in the middle of the rear seat. He smiled. "How are you doing, Dr. Stefanelli?"

"Much better, thank you, Mr. Secretary." She paused for a moment. "Is that still the correct form of address?"

"For the next few hours it'll do just fine." Ben Levy smiled and drove on.

Minutes later the Mercedes pulled to a stop down the street from a little bar on Connecticut Ave, where a tall man in a trenchcoat paced nonchalantly outside the covered entrance.

He had a trimmed beard and wire-rim glasses. "Have a good evening," he greeted a couple as they were leaving the tavern. When he saw the Mercedes he hustled over to it. Stewart was already on the sidewalk helping Nina and the maids climb out.

The man swooped behind them and slid into the back of the car. "They have a big screen TV in there," he called out. "Enjoy the show." He swung the door closed.

"Come on," Stewart ordered, leading the women away. The rain was getting heavier.

"Who was that?" Nina wanted to know, glancing at the car as the driver checked traffic.

"Just another guy with something to get off his chest," Stewart told her. He kept them moving towards the tavern at a fast pace. The Mercedes pulled away briskly.

39

Foster recalled reading somewhere that Bulgarian dissident Georgi Markov was assassinated in the late 70s with a tiny pellet shot into his leg. The British doctors who performed the autopsy discovered a coating of ricin on the pellet. Ricin, he knew, is highly toxic – some 6,000 times more so than cyanide. It's also odorless, tasteless, and water-soluble.

Ricin, in other words, would be the perfect additive for Stewart's morning cup of coffee.

Foster had just finished talking to the backstabber on his cell phone. The bastard had double-crossed him, and now he had to deliver the news personally to the world's most powerful man, who was standing some twenty feet away with his chief advisor in the staging area of the media room. He moved with sickening reluctance in their direction, furious that he had let a dolt like Stewart trick him.

"I just talked to Stewart," he announced to the president, his tongue searching his mouth for saliva that wasn't there.

"Mathews' wife was taken to an offsite treatment center for shock rehabilitation. She won't be coming back tonight."

Hawkins purpled. "Stewart let her leave?! Who took her?!"

"He didn't say. He said Fann Li has agreed to read the statement for her."

"Fann Li?!" Gage croaked. "Fann Li?! Get Stewart! Tell him to get that other bitch here now! I don't care if she's dead! Tell Fann Li to go back to her floor mat!"

"He reminded me Fanny has TV aspirations and will probably deliver the message better than Stefanelli. Sir, she's in the audience with the reporters and looks confident. Her Asian features will go over well. Stefanelli was too European."

"We don't make changes like this at the last second!" Gage could barely summon the lung power to speak. "Stefanelli was Mathews' wife. Fann Li—. The whole point—" He stopped to catch his breath. "We have—"

"—One minute, Mr. President!" a TV technician called to him.

"—no use for an Asian imp to make a statement about Mathews' stunts."

"Sir, I—"

"We're short on time," Hawkins interrupted. "Li won't say anything disruptive, and she might help. I say go with her."

"We'll go with her," Gage said. "And when this is over I'll go with new advisors."

"My name is Fann Li, and I am honored to be here this evening," she began, standing behind a wooden lectern she could scarcely see over. "As an Asian-American who hopes for a brighter tomorrow for all people, I implore Preston Mathews to cease his interventions into our economic lives and speak with our elected representatives in a responsible manner. . ."

She didn't mess up once. Gage applauded her as he took her place behind the lectern. Hawkins, who was out of camera range on the dais, clapped politely as she passed by him. He kept his face pleasantly blank. "Thank you, Ms. Li," Gage said to the country. "As some of you may know, Ms. Li works as a private contractor in the field of physical therapy, and I wanted the American people to hear from someone outside of government on the Preston Mathews issue. Those of you who may believe Dr. Mathews has an issue only with government need to rethink their positions. As we heard her say, his disruptions are affecting all Americans – you, me, her, and countless others. He has caused economic hardships throughout our society, not just for big investors and bankers. He apparently has supporters who have computer and networking expertise and believe anything goes when it comes to supporting the cause.

"But let me make this clear: Preston Mathews is a good man at heart. I've known him for years, and I can tell you with certainty that he wants nothing but the best for the American people. To achieve his goal he left the private sector a few years ago and moved into government service, where he served as chairman of the organization that he now finds so problematic. Quite frankly, I wouldn't be surprised if he's identified difficulties within the Federal Reserve System that need to be addressed soon, and I and others in my administration, as well as Congress, are eager to work with him to arrive at responsible solutions. So, I call on Dr. Mathews, wherever he is, to make himself . . . available for . . ."

A commotion was building up among the reporters. Gage took his eyes off the teleprompter and saw Levy and Mathews standing in the audience against the wall to Gage's right, politely attentive to the president's remarks. They had slipped in while Gage was reading his message. They were both in suits, and Mathews, his disguise gone, looked like his old Fed chairman self.

"Well, we have quite a surprise this evening," Gage said, clearing his throat. Hawkins was waving his arms frantically to get his attention but to no avail. "None other than Preston Mathews himself has entered the room, along with Treasury Secretary Ben Levy. I don't know what prompted Dr. Mathews to join us, but I'm glad he is here and would like to ask him—" Gage turned and saw Hawkins emphatically and repeatedly drawing his hand across his throat to nix any notion of an ad lib. After a moment's hesitation Gage turned back to the reporters and the TV cameras. "—I would like to ask him if he would speak to the American people and perhaps clear up some of the confusion. How about it, Dr. Mathews? Will you step to the dais for a minute?"

Mathews smiled and came up onstage. The camera followed him. The TV audience saw him pause for a handshake with Hawkins.

"We know where your wife is, Mathews."

"That's more than I can say about yours."

Mathews smiled then went over and shook hands with Gage, who then surrendered the lectern. Mathews went behind it, reconsidered, then came around front. He looked like a youngster who had just returned from an exhilarating adventure. Gage had the confused look of a man who had lost his bearings.

"Thank you, Mr. President, for giving me this opportunity to speak," Mathews began.

**40**

"It wasn't so long ago that I stood before a TV camera as Chairman of the Board of Governors of the Federal Reserve System telling you inflation was under control and the economy was strong and getting better. Then I walked off the set and a week later deliberately crashed my biplane at a certain spot on the farm I own. The plane exploded into flames in front of my barn, where I had painted a graphic depicting the secret life of our currency. I had rendered an image of the federal reserve one dollar bill, with a skull and crossbones replacing the picture of George Washington, because the money we use is an instrument of theft, war, and enslavement – which is appropriate for pirates, not our first president. The government knows it. The Federal Reserve knows it. And I wanted you to know it so you could help stop the horrors it funds.

"The flight, the crash, and the image were all calculated to get your attention. I wanted to alert you to a grave danger, that our money, and therefore our society as we know it, is headed for catastrophe. Rather than wait for the crisis to arrive and let government 'do something' to make it worse, I wanted to build a base of supporters who would demand a new monetary standard untainted by government involvement. My point is this: the fiat dollars we've been forced to use for over 70 years have had an insidious effect on our lives and threaten to destroy us if we don't return to sound money."

Gage directed his gaze at Levy, expecting to see outrage or confusion or both over Mathews' comments. When he saw instead a satisfied grin, he had only one thought: Levy had turned. The bastard was a traitor. Levy had been Mathews' free pass to the press room. Stopping Mathews now would be disastrous. Not stopping him would be disastrous. Gage's only chance for a propaganda victory would be to confute Mathews' idiocies after he was done blathering. At least Gage would have the last word, the only word most of his listeners would remember. He found himself looking around the room for Stewart, where the big dope would no doubt be all mushy from this sudden effrontery. Here was the president of the United States, back in high school, debating ideas as if they were important in the real world . . .

"Though it won't be easy to do," Mathews continued, "we need to (1) make government stop increasing the supply of dollars and repeal all legal tender laws; (2) deactivate the federal reserve system in preparation for abolishing it altogether; and (3) reclaim the gold held by the Treasury by having banks convert all federal reserve notes and bank deposits into gold coin. If we are to establish a sound monetary system, the dollar must be denationalized and severed from government completely. It must become a name for a certain weight of gold, or even better, the dollar and every other name for a currency should be dropped and prices expressed as a weight – grams or ounces, say – of a precious metal, such as gold or silver.

"This, I admit, is a radical proposal, but we're dealing with a radical problem. There will be hardships, but there is no painless path to honest money and banking. And those of you familiar with the monetary meltdowns of other economies, such as Germany and Yugoslavia, know that the longer we wait, the greater the pain. How bad is a monetary meltdown? As economics professor Steve Hanke put it, ask yourself what you could buy if the government took your bank account and moved the decimal point 22 places to the left. That's what happened to Yugoslavia in the early 1990s.

"Yugoslavia and Germany present examples of runaway inflation, where during the meltdown's late stages the value of the currency drops so fast it ceases to function as a medium of exchange. But as the history of central banking and fiat money makes clear, we don't need a runaway inflation to create hell on earth. Ordinary inflation will do just fine.

"Let me pause here for a confession." And here he did pause for what would be the most difficult part of his speech. "It's not easy to admit to deception, but you should hear it from me and judge accordingly. I've known the truth of these matters since long before I accepted the post as Fed chairman, but saw no way to bring about honest money and banking without initiating a movement from the inside, at the top. As Fed chairman, therefore, I was head of a system I knew to be wrong and disastrous. Along with my colleagues on the board, I conducted policy on the assumption that our future depended on a dying dollar. Our decisions on interest rates pushed the dollar closer to extinction. The media was fixed on the interest rates themselves, or unemployment, or the CPI, or some other macro-measure of economic health. It never once identified us as professional inflationists. But that's what we were. And I've known it all along. The media, your supposed guardians, never gazed at the increasingly depreciated dollar and asked, 'What the hell's going on?!'

"There should be a sign on the front of the Fed building in Washington saying, 'We work for the elites – the commercial bankers and government – at the expense of everyone else. Try and stop us.'

"Let's try, shall we?

"Bankers and politicians have had a mutually rewarding relationship for ages. Bankers create money and loan it out at interest, which can be very profitable. Trouble is, creating money electronically or with a printing press, which is what central banks do, is counterfeiting. In return for a share of the newly-created money, government lets banks get away with it. Government gets bigger, bankers get richer.

"Bank counterfeiting, which is another name for inflation, fuels a great many evils for which it gets little credit, such as wars and depressions. To put an end to this racket we need to establish a free market in banking, which means open it up to competition. What would prevent banks from counterfeiting on a free market? Property right enforcement. All money is someone's property. If I deposit my money in a bank and pay a fee for the service, I expect to be able to get it back on demand. If the bank can't provide it because the bank's loaned it to someone else, it has violated my property rights. If the law respects property rights consistently, the law will hold the bank responsible. In the long run at least, counterfeiting would be unprofitable. Few bankers will find such prospects tempting.

"Money was founded on the market. At first it was a commodity that was bartered for other commodities or services. But because of the great number of people willing to accept it in trade, it began to be acquired for trading purposes only – as a medium of exchange, or money. Gold won the competition as the most popular money long ago. Gold is very difficult to produce, which is one of the biggest reasons it became the preferred medium of exchange. When a rare commodity such as gold is used for money, the supply remains fairly constant. People have always known that increasing the money supply dilutes the value of each monetary unit. But apparently they didn't make a connection between this fact and government's eagerness to adopt a fiat dollar as our monetary standard. When new money is created as a matter of policy, as it has been for generations with the encouragement of leading economists, the dollar is doomed, and so are dollar users.

"We need to remember, though, that banking as such is crucial to higher civilization. As one commentator has astutely observed, without an international banking system most of us wouldn't be alive today. Money and banking make possible the division of labor, which has drastically reduced child mortality and raised living standards wherever free markets flourished.  But it's also true that throughout most of banking history, banks promised to redeem their notes in some precious metal, either gold or silver.  Though they could keep that promise for only a small fraction of their customers, it still served as a vital check on their propensity to counterfeit.

"For Americans, the gold standard was killed by presidential decree during the crisis of the Great Depression.  In 1971 another president told foreigners they could no longer get gold for American dollars and thus removed the last trace of monetary gold from international trade.  Since then all governments have been on a fiat money standard, depreciating their currencies as a matter of policy.

"The story of gold's disappearance is part of a larger narrative about the growth of government.  Besides being a check on bank counterfeiting, or inflation, gold is also a serious restriction on government expansion.  For the advocates of big government, therefore, gold becomes a barbarous relic that stands in their way.

"The corruption of money began when people started keeping their gold with banks, which would issue deposit receipts, or banknotes, as money-substitutes.  Because of the banker's reputation for trust and propriety, their notes were readily acceptable in trade as substitutes for the gold locked away in their vaults.  People knew they could redeem the notes for gold any time they wished.  But because of the convenience of carrying and doing business with banknotes rather than coins, people tended to leave their gold in the bank.

"Bankers became the money centers of their communities, even though most of the money under their protection wasn't theirs – they could only claim a small percentage of it as a fee for their service. Because money was in their possession, though, businessmen would come to them for loans, and the bankers, seeking additional profit opportunities, found ways to accommodate them.

"Unfortunately, they turned to counterfeiting as a means of accommodation. What I mean is, they began creating and loaning out deposit receipts that had no gold behind them. The new notes were counterfeit because they were being passed off with the understanding that they were genuine gold substitutes. But in fact the notes only looked like the real thing. The bankers knew, though, that as long as they didn't issue too many of these counterfeit bills, they would escape detection.

"In extending loans with counterfeit notes or by creating unbacked deposit accounts, they could point to conspicuous growth in the local economy. According to almost everything we read, bankers weren't committing fraud, they were helping business grow, putting people to work, helping them earn a living. As businessmen, the bankers could tell themselves they were merely reacting to the demands of the market, in their case a demand for money. And they reacted by simply printing and issuing it.

"Looking back, most commentators now find little fault with what they were doing. So what if their notes weren't backed by gold? Today's financial press would say the bankers were 'investing' or 'accommodating' or 'providing liquidity.' You never hear anyone call it counterfeiting, at least not in mainstream circles.

"But by issuing banknotes or credit not covered by gold, the bankers were increasing the money supply, a process

identical in its effects to counterfeiting.  An increase in the
supply of money confers no broad social benefits – but it does
benefit early users of the new money at the expense of others:
the first users have the advantage of buying goods at current
prices.  Later, when prices have gone up, the inflated money
supply doesn't benefit anyone.  We improve the general
welfare by increasing the production of goods, not by
increasing the production of money.

"Nevertheless, the banks' practice of generating unbacked
money substitutes prevailed.  Invariably, some would go too
far and cause depositors to begin doubting their banker's
rectitude.  A few would start showing up at teller windows
wanting their notes exchanged for gold.  Other note holders
would catch on, and the bank was soon confronted with a run.
But without enough gold to redeem, many of the banks had to
shut their doors.  As the panic spread, even the more cautious
banks would experience massive demands for redemption.

"For reasons of its own, government took a strong interest
in the bankers' plight and usually issued moratoriums on note
redemption.  For a period sometimes lasting years, banks were
permitted to default on their liabilities to note holders while
being allowed to conduct all other banking activities.

"Helpful as this privilege was, it wasn't enough.  Banks
weren't always allowed to renege on their promises, their easy
credit policies created bankruptcies and recessions, and
besides, bank runs were embarrassing.  No banker liked seeing
crowds swarming at his door demanding what was theirs,
even if the law was on his side.

"Fortunately for American bankers and their political
allies, Europe provided examples of ingenious solutions to the

dilemma of bank counterfeiting. During the early years of the twentieth century U. S. bankers imported some of their ideas and, together with a few powerful politicians, devised a plan for a banking cartel.

"The cartel would consist of all the national banks of the country organized under the authority of a central bank, which would be endowed by government with a monopoly of the note issue. Furthermore, all the deposits of the member banks would be moved to the central bank and held as reserves, with the central bank dictating to its members what fraction of its reserves they had to maintain when making loans. Historically, banks have been held to a ten percent reserve requirement most of the time, meaning they could extend nine dollars in loans for every dollar held in reserve. By dictating reserve ratios for all members, the central bank would control the rate of monetary inflation in a uniform manner so that any one bank wouldn't get more reckless than the others and get itself and the rest of the banks in trouble.

"Americans didn't like cartels or centralized power, the planners realized, so they called their creature a 'reserve system' instead of a banking cartel and dressed it up with regional branches to avoid the appearance of a concentration of power. As John Kenneth Galbraith observed many years later, the regional design was ingenious for serving local pride 'and for lulling the suspicions of the agrarians.' Since no cartel will work without government guns, it was natural, perhaps, to attach the name 'federal' to it, as well. Thus, the American central bank became known as the Federal Reserve System, or the Fed.

"Signed into law on December 23, 1913, the Federal Reserve Act was hailed as a major victory of the Progressive Era's fight against the alleged abuses of concentrated market power, in this case, the Money Trust. Banking was at last rescued from the hands of Wall Street and put under the enlightened care of government. Greed had been tamed by the people through their selfless representatives in Congress and their man in the White House. Government would see that the Fed served the 'public interest' and would ensure that it didn't fail. And with the Fed providing the economy with an 'elastic currency,' the ruinous panics and depressions of the past would be gone forever.

"Those were the beliefs, but the facts reveal a far different story.

"It was the Morgans and Rockefellers of Wall Street who turned to government to cage their banking competition, especially the growing challenge from non-national banks in the South and West, and came up with a plan for a central bank. It was the big bankers who took the lead in creating a system that would protect them from the hazards of bank counterfeiting and make them a monopoly issuer of bank notes. After the Act became law, it was Morgan bankers who occupied the seats of power in the new system, particularly at the Fed's New York branch where Benjamin Strong, president of J. P. Morgan's Bankers Trust Company, ran the money machine from the Fed's inception in 1914 to his death in 1928.

"The Fed became an indispensable instrument of profit and power. Beginning in 1914, it cut reserve requirements approximately in half, dropping the ratio from 21 percent to 11 percent, roughly doubling the money supply and permitting both financial aid to the Allies and eventual American entry into the European war. Under the impetus of the war, the Fed became the sole fiscal agent of the Treasury, securing the deposit of all Treasury funds at the Federal Reserve. The Morgans, exploiting its ties with England and its position of power at the New York Fed, became the sole purchasing agent in the U.S. for war materials to be shipped to Britain and France. The Morgans also became the sole underwriter for British and French bonds floated in the U.S. to pay for armaments and other goods the Allies wanted.

"Government, meanwhile, used the war as an excuse to create what one economic historian has aptly called a 'garrison economy.' Among other things government took over railroads and communications industries, seized hundreds of manufacturing plants, fixed prices, intervened in hundreds of labor disputes, raised taxes, and conscripted a million men for military service so they could join the bloodbath *over there*, in the European trenches. The Supreme Court, the alleged guardian of the Constitution – which itself is our alleged guardian against an aggressive government – ruled most of the war interventions constitutional, including the draft. Merely questioning the constitutionality of the draft could get you thrown in jail. Thus, the federal reserve – a government-protected, government-serving, elaborately-cloaked counterfeiting cartel – played a crucial role in converting a peaceful America into a bellicose, interventionist state.

"All the belligerents in the war went off the gold standard and resorted to inflation – counterfeiting – to fund the carnage. Taxes were raised, but only so far. Governments that attempt to fund wars by raising taxes often find themselves facing a revolt on the home front. Wars require massive inflation, and the institution responsible for inflation is the government's central bank. Without government control of the monetary system through its central bank there would've been no war, or certainly not one nearly as long or destructive.

"The war killed over 19 million people, counting both military and civilian deaths. How many of those deaths could have been prevented if the governments did not control the money supplies? If they had engaged in central bank 'disarmament' instead of slaughtering one another?

"Rather than pointing out the inflationary theft of resources that underlies all modern wars, many commentators were instead spellbound by the patriotic fervor and the wonderful command and control economy the war brought in its wake. No doubt it was a heady experience for the elites in command and very lucrative for a few others. In this connection I strongly urge you to read a short book written by two-time Medal of Honor recipient, Major General Smedley D. Butler, called *War is a Racket*. A racket, General Butler said, is something that is not what it seems to the majority of people. Only a small group of insiders knows what it is about. A racket is conducted for the benefit of the very few at the expense of the very many.

"We hear voices calling for patriotism during war. But who exactly were the patriots during 'the war to end all wars'? Was it J. P. Morgan, who repeatedly said, 'Nobody could hate war more than I do' as he was amassing commissions totaling $30 million as a purchasing agent of war supplies for England and France? Was it Morgan's steel, shipbuilding, and powder enterprises that bought controlling interest in, and editorial control over, the country's 25 most influential newspapers? Was it President Woodrow Wilson who had won reelection with the slogan 'he kept us out of war' then five months later asked Congress to join a war that had already killed 5 million men? Was it Senator Robert La Follette of Wisconsin, who rose in the Senate to dissect Wilson's call for war point by point, arguing that Wilson and his advisors had been colluding with Britain for two years trying to find a pretext for American entry into the fray against England's enemies? Was it the senators who spoke after La Follette and for five hours hotly denounced him as 'pro-German' and 'anti-American'? Was it the majority of Americans who in spite of a well-orchestrated media campaign against Germany still opposed joining the war? Was it the million men who were conscripted and sent overseas, over 100,000 of whom lost their lives? Was it the industrial firms back home, thousands of miles from the slaughter on the Western Front, whose income tax records showed huge profits during the war years? Was it the millions here who kept their mouths shut about the war because the Espionage Act of 1917 and its successor, the Sedition Act of 1918, hung a 20-year prison sentence over the heads of Wilson's critics?

"Washington, Jefferson, Madison, and John Quincy Adams are generally considered patriotic, yet they counseled strongly against American entanglement in foreign affairs. 'Commerce with all nations, alliance with none,' were Jefferson's famous words. America 'well knows that by once enlisting under other banners than her own, the fundamental maxims of her policies would insensibly change from liberty to force,' John Quincy Adams warned his colleagues in a famous Fourth of July speech to Congress. 'Of all the enemies of true liberty,' James Madison wrote, 'war is, perhaps, the most to be dreaded, because it comprises and develops the germ of every other. War is the parent of armies; from these proceed debts and taxes; and armies, and debts, and taxes are the known instruments for bringing the many under the domination of the few.'

"The Fed, and its partner in theft, the income tax, enabled politicians and their financial backers to ignore their warnings. Should we be surprised that many American war supporters made out like bandits? J. P. Morgan was one of those Americans who cleaned up handsomely from the war he professed to hate. As journalist H. L. Mencken noted a few years later, 'The Government hospitals are now full of one-legged soldiers who gallantly protected [Morgan's] investments then, and the public schools are full of boys who will protect his investments tomorrow.'

"The man who unfortunately became the most influential inflationist of the twentieth century, John Maynard Keynes, saw clearly how monetary fraud leads to a country's downfall. Writing shortly after World War I, he said, 'There is no subtler, no surer means of overturning the existing basis of society than to debauch the currency. The process engages all the hidden forces of economic law on the side of destruction, and does it in a manner which not one man in a million is able to diagnose.' To 'debauch' a currency you inflate it.

"No government bent on amassing power, however, can do so while banknotes and deposits are still redeemable in gold.  Gold, therefore, has to go, but it must be removed in a deceptive manner, so that people won't notice the theft. Encouraging people to keep their gold in banks is a crucial first step on the road to confiscation, but having it reside in local banks means people can withdraw it easily.  The next step, therefore, is to create or exploit a crisis and cite that as an excuse to have it moved into the vaults of the central government.  In theory, it would still be accessible to the owners, but highly inconvenient and, not coincidentally, unpatriotic to withdraw.

"Thus, in 1917 the Federal Reserve law was changed to allow the Fed to exchange its notes for gold, on the grounds that the government wanted to protect the gold supply from foreigners.  In dealing with its member banks the Fed increased its holdings from 28 percent of the nation's gold stock before American entry into the war to 74 percent by the war's end.  With gold largely centralized at the Fed, people were reluctant to touch it.  Instead, they dealt almost exclusively with notes that promised to pay gold coin on demand.

"After the war, and after a depression from 1920 to 1921 made brief by government's inability to intervene in time, the Fed continued its inflationary policies and financed the boom years of the 1920s.  Most economists today will tell you we had no inflation during this decade because overall prices remained the same.  But the 1920s were also a period of advancing technology and new methods of manufacturing, which improved productivity enough to hold prices level.  In other words, if the banks had not engaged in credit expansion during the '20s, prices would've dropped, and the country would have enjoyed prosperity without a crash waiting in the wings. But in fact the Fed boosted the money supply by roughly $26 billion from mid-1922 to mid-1929. And the new money pushed stock and real estate prices up to feverish levels.

"The stock market break that began in October, 1929 signaled the beginning of a necessary correction to the preceding boom years. From the country's first major depression in 1819 until the depression of the early 1920s, government had mostly allowed the economy to correct itself. The depressions, consequently, lasted only about a year or two, and 1930 should have been a typical period of correction and gradual recovery.

"The country's failure to recover is unfairly blamed on the Federal Reserve, which is charged with failing to initiate an inflationary binge to restore the lost euphoria. The Fed certainly tried to inflate the economy back to the boom by lowering interest rates and purchasing government securities, and it deserves blame for the Crash itself because of the money it created. But it was government intervention that deepened and prolonged the depression.

"To repeat, credit expansion brought on the Crash, government policies lengthened and intensified the depression.

"On the surface, the goals of the interventionists had a noble ring – they were being done to keep wage rates and prices from falling. Thus, for example, the Hawley-Smoot Tariff of June, 1930 was promoted as a way to support domestic industry and labor, but it virtually closed foreign markets to American products. Agriculture, a major export industry, was hit particularly hard, and prices for farm products dropped to unprecedented lows. Hundreds of thousands of farmers went into bankruptcy, and the rural banks who were their creditors suffered the consequences. From 1930 to 1933, many thousands of banks failed. The crushing blow to agriculture caused great harm to the banking system, which in turn spread panic to its millions of customers.

"The Hoover administration did everything it could to revive the economy, which was precisely why economic conditions grew worse. They believed the command economy installed for World War I had been effective in putting the U.S. on the winning side. If government controls were successful during a war, why not put government in charge of a receding economy? Having abandoned the teachings of the classical liberals, they believed that government decrees had produced the goods that won the war. Another round of government impositions, they were convinced, would again make the desired outcome appear.

"'We could have done nothing,' Hoover said during his 1932 presidential campaign, but 'that would have been utter ruin.' He attacked those economists who had urged a hands-off approach, claiming he was determined not to 'follow the advice of the bitter-end liquidationists ,' as he disparagingly called them, and see the whole body of debtors and savers 'brought to destruction.'

"But he only intensified the destruction he sought to avoid. Liquidation of unsound projects created by the inflationary boom was precisely the tonic needed to revive the economy, as history and theory had made clear. When he left office, his coercive concern for the whole body of debtors and savers left one in four workers unemployed, a new low in American history.

"And yet, incredibly, we find historians and economists describing Hoover's policies as 'laissez-faire,' as if he sat back and did nothing while the economy tried to correct itself. If only he had. He intervened far more than any president before him and brought the economy to its knees. Government should 'do something' was the dominant thinking then as now, and applying the laissez-faire label pinned the blame on the market instead of the government. If Hoover had been re-elected, he might have been even more aggressive in attacking the economy. As it was, he left that to his successor.

"In his inaugural address the new U.S. president told the American people their economic problems were due to 'unscrupulous money changers' whose conduct in banking and business was 'callous' and 'selfish.' He promised his listeners that if Congress should fail to act properly, he would ask them for broad executive powers that might be given to a president in the event of an invasion. One Supreme Court justice described the depression as 'an emergency more serious than war.' Taking the hint, Congress acceded to the president's wish and granted him dictatorial powers to resolve the banking crisis.

"After his inaugural address Roosevelt issued Presidential Proclamation 2039 in which he explained the cause of the national emergency as the 'heavy and unwarranted withdrawals of gold and currency from our banking institutions for the purpose of hoarding,' along with speculation abroad in foreign exchange that 'has resulted in severe drains on the Nation's stocks of gold.' Gold and hoarding were his targets. 'It is in the best interests of all bank depositors,' he concluded, 'that a period of respite be provided' to prevent 'further hoarding of coin, bullion or currency or speculation in foreign exchange.' He concluded the proclamation by closing all banks in 1933 from March 6 to March 9, inclusive.

"Hoarding is a pejorative term for an increase in an individual's cash holdings. If hoarders are guilty of anything, it's for exposing the unscrupulous and unsound nature of the banking system for manufacturing multiple claims to the same deposit of gold. In 1931, as people were redeeming $800 million in bank deposits for cash, Hoover lashed out at them for their 'traitorous hoarding.' In early 1932 he organized a citizens committee and launched a public campaign against hoarders, blaming them for keeping the country mired in the depression by withholding money from circulation. Evidently, Roosevelt and his Brain Trust agreed with him. But people, in taking their money out of the banks, were only trying to protect what was rightfully theirs. There would have been no problems with hoarding had the bankers not been cheating them.

"We need to remember that money is a medium of exchange and not wealth as such, and the act of withdrawing deposits and keeping them off the market, which decreases the money supply, does not destroy wealth. It only means each monetary unit will command more resources than before. In other words, prices will drop.

"But as we saw, falling prices and wages had been the devil government was fighting. Government spokesmen had reversed cause and effect – at least in their public statements. Rather than seeing the depression as causing prices and wages to drop, they credulously proclaimed that lower prices and wages caused the depression, ignoring ample historical evidence to the contrary. By their logic, therefore, bringing the country out of the depression was a matter of boosting prices and wages to where they were during the good times before the Crash. Since 'hoarding' was keeping this from happening, on April 5, 1933 Roosevelt ordered all people with gold in their possession to turn it over to the Federal Reserve, for which they would receive government paper money in return. Who could pass up a deal like that? The government figured everyone could, so they made it a felony for failing to comply, punishable by a fine not exceeding $10,000 and a prison sentence of up to 10 years.

"In its eagerness to inflate the money supply, government was busy inflating the criminal supply. People, in other words, were becoming criminals only because they were resisting the criminality of the state. One of our foremost economic commentators cites the famous work of Friedman and Schwartz, *A Monetary History of the United States, 1867-1960*, in pointing out that many American citizens anticipated Roosevelt's gold confiscation and successfully kept their property from the state's greedy hands. During the three months prior to Roosevelt's gold grab, circulating gold coin diminished by a whopping 35.5 percent. The state's actual theft was only 3.9 million ounces or 22 percent of the gold coin then in circulation. Friedman and Schwartz conclude that the remaining 78 percent – roughly 13.9 million ounces of gold – "was retained illegally in private hands." I commend those people who resisted the plunder, whoever they were.

"If it had been possible to print gold, government would never have abandoned the gold standard. But it did, and the alleged evil preventing recovery was eliminated by presidential decree. Government now had a money machine with virtually no brakes. They could inflate the money supply as necessary, drive prices and wages up, and put people back to work.

"Things didn't go exactly as planned and another World War had to start – and end – before the economy returned to its pre-Crash condition. The private economy got a big boost after the war when government cut spending by two-thirds from 1945 to 1948, and wartime price controls and rationing of consumer goods were lifted. Keynesian economists predicted another depression when government spending was slashed. They had also predicted government spending would lift the economy out of the depression during the 1930s.

"What happened in the 1930s to prevent economic recovery? In a word, government.

"The New Deal, with its barrage of regulations and bureaucracies, increased the burdens of business, lowering productivity and discouraging expansion. The New Deal gave special favors to organized labor, increasing wages for union members but making it more difficult for businesses to hire the unemployed.

"In mid-1935 and early 1936 the Supreme Court killed the two centerpieces of New Deal legislation, the National

Industrial Recovery Act and the Agricultural Adjustment Act. With less government on their backs, Americans began to make the economy grow. From August, 1935 to May, 1937 production, private-sector employment, and stock prices rose. But in August, 1937 the economy started an uninterrupted downward slide, with the Dow losing 90 points by March 31, 1938. What went wrong?

"Most commentators, including many with an otherwise free market orientation, place the blame squarely on the federal reserve. The Fed raised bank reserve requirements by 50 percent in August, 1936, while announcing two more increases of 25 percent each the following year. With reserve requirements increased, credit was tighter, and the recovering economy couldn't get the money it needed to continue growing, it is argued.

"If tight credit is the culprit, we would expect commercial lending to decrease, but that didn't happen. From the third quarter of 1935 through the end of 1937, commercial loans of member banks soared – from $4.8 billion to nearly $7 billion. But didn't the increased reserve requirements raise interest rates, you might ask? Yes, they raised them 'from levels absurdly low to levels still absurdly low,' as Chase National Bank's chief economist during this period, Benjamin Anderson, has observed. The deflationary actions of the Fed, in other words, did not discourage business borrowing.

"What caused the economic recovery to collapse? The same policies that prolonged and deepened the Depression.

"Roosevelt was bitter about the recovery because it was proceeding over the dead body of his cherished NRA. With advice from Harvard law professor Felix Frankfurter, he began considering an amendment to the Constitution that would allow him to pack the Court to his liking. Other advisers urged him to heighten his attack on big business and on the wealthy, whom he labeled 'economic royalists.'

"And so Roosevelt hit harder at business, and business responded with a slump.

"Britain, France, and other European countries had also abandoned gold in the early 1930s and saw their international economic order thrown into chaos. With fluctuating fiat currencies doing battle with one another, international investment and trade virtually disappeared. The United States, because of its policy of redeeming dollars for gold for foreign governments and central banks, became a relatively safe monetary haven and found itself inundated with gold from abroad.

"The governments of the United States and Europe longed for the stability of the international gold standard of the 19th century – but without the gold. Their official position was and still is that gold and the free market caused the Depression. No one in power championed the classical gold standard, much less a gold standard uncorrupted by government. The mixed economy, with government determining the mix, became a synonym for the market economy, at least in Establishment discussions. And a market economy could be anything short of full socialism. Any perceived problem with the economy, therefore, became another failing of the market and required more government intervention to fix. The continuing difficulty with money and inflation required careful government tinkering.

"In 1944 representatives from the Allied nations met at the Bretton Woods Hotel in New Hampshire and worked out an agreement wherein the American dollar was declared as good as gold.  Thereafter, signatories to this agreement would use American dollars as their reserve currency, and the United States, loaded with gold, promised to continue its policy of redeeming gold to foreigners.

"The United States inflated freely after the war, and U.S. government aid to Europe and increased U.S. imports piled up American dollars in European banks.  As the piles grew larger, the dollar lost value, and the Europeans, particularly France and de Gaulle's gold-standard advisor, Jacques Rueff, complained about being tied to an arrangement that was harming their economic interests.  When the U.S. rejected their complaints out of hand, European governments began exercising their option of redeeming dollars for gold at $35 an ounce.  The U.S. pressured them to desist, but U.S. inflation continued, and so did the cashing in of American dollars.  Finally, on August 15, 1971, with the U.S. gold supply continuing its flight overseas, President Nixon took the U.S. off the gold standard completely, refusing to honor the Bretton Woods agreement of 1944.

"For the first time since the founding of the republic the dollar was completely divorced from its precious metal origin.  It now joined the ranks of other major currencies as a purely fiat money.

"With gold no longer money even to foreigners, what restrains Fed inflation today?  Not much.  The dollar's competition with other inflated currencies is one restraint.  Most of you have heard of the Consumer Price Index and its inadequacies in measuring inflation's effect on prices. Yet it helps restrain the money machine somewhat, as does the market price of gold. But unlike a gold standard, in no case do any of these restraints directly threaten the Fed's ability to stay in operation. The Federal Reserve System markets a dangerous and shoddy product, the fiat dollar, or what I call the Jolly Roger dollar, but since it's legal tender we have little choice but to use it. Government and the banks profit handsomely from this arrangement. And we accept it because this is what all governments and their central banks do. And we're told this is a necessary and good thing.

"And it is – for those in power who benefit from this scheme.

"Have you noticed we've been at war almost constantly since the Fed was forced upon us? We had World War I, the Great Depression, which was likened to war by the rulers, World War II, then the umbrella of the Cold War under which two hot wars and various skirmishes were fought. And now the endless war on terrorism. For a president eager to go to war, the Fed has been a godsend.

"Smedley Butler said war is a racket. It is. And so is the Fed. Two rackets, both aligned against Americans for the benefit of a privileged few. Presidents lie us into war while media minions cheer them on. But before the carnage can proceed very far the government needs money, lots of it, more than it gets through taxation. And the loyal Fed is there to provide 'accommodation.' The Federal Reserve makes war seem affordable. The media makes war seem patriotic. And in the background, waiting to be fattened, are the politicians' corporate supporters who profit hugely from foreign invasions.

"Have you noticed the economic trends since the Fed took over the money supply? The Fed was supposed to protect the value of the dollar and spare us from economic crises. The dollar today is approaching collapse, and economic calamities live on. Should we be surprised at these outcomes? Of course not. The Fed was designed to inflate. Inflation depreciates the dollar. Inflation fuels economic crises by misleading investors.

"If we truly desire peace and prosperity, we will wipe every trace of central banking and fiat money from the face of the earth. Fiat currencies always bring out the worst in government as it inflates us into war, economic ruin, and autocratic rule.

"Those of you who are young, think about your future. Or if you're the parent or grandparent of young people, think about theirs. We are faced with a choice – war and inflation, or peace and prosperity. Repressive government and cartels, or limited government and open markets. Central banking and fiat money, or competitive banking and gold.

"The president said earlier I want only the best for the American people. That is a profoundly true statement. And the best in monetary affairs is a gold standard with full reserve banking. It's not only the best, it's our only hope for restoring peace, prosperity, and liberty. It's for that reason, and that reason only, that I've been fighting for gold. I ask that you join me in this fight.

"That is all I have to say for now, but with the president's permission I would like to invite Secretary Levy to the podium for a few comments."

Gage was in a quiet state of shock. Mathews stepped down and let Levy take the lectern.

"We don't need it replaced with something 'fair,'" he said without prelude. "We need it eliminated. I'm talking about the income tax, of course. It needs to go, as does government spending. The only people who should be spending are the legitimate owners of wealth. Stealing wealth doesn't make us legitimate owners, even if the thieves are duly elected. Taxes are theft. *Taxes are theft*. Is there such a thing as a 'fair' tax? No. A 'fair' tax is no more possible than a 'fair' theft. That's something I knew but wouldn't allow myself to accept until a little while ago. A 'fair' tax is an oxymoron. Since that is most definitely not the guiding philosophy of the U.S. Treasury, I am unfit to lead it – never was fit, really – and hereby announce my resignation. Thank you."

**41**

Gage watched them return to their original positions along the wall. His skull was splitting but he barely noticed. He moved behind the lectern and glared at the two interlopers.

"I would like to make one thing clear. And that is this: Anyone who finds so much wrong with America and its way of life should do himself and us a big favor and get the hell out." He paused, and the reporters present exploded with a boisterous ovation. "I apologize for using profane language, but I feel strongly about this issue."

He was interrupted with more applause, then went on to talk about the great blessings of American government, including all its wars fought for freedom, how it helps the poor and oppressed, and how it makes Americans stand tall in the world. "Given the tasks Americans have assigned to their government, the revenue we collect is rightfully ours, much as the money owed for an electric bill is rightfully the electric company's. People don't talk seriously about the power company 'stealing' their money, so why should they talk that way about taxes and government deficits? To repeat, the dollars we withhold from your paychecks are rightfully ours. And the national debt we incur to cover our revenue shortfall is a wash because we owe it to ourselves. We don't need to turn the clock back, we don't need to throw government out the window, we need to support what we have because it works! And I know most Americans are with me because a majority of voters voted me into office. . ."

A young guard who saw Hawkins leave the media room told FBI investigators later that Gage's Chief of Staff appeared to be a man who had lost his bearings. "I knew from his face something really bad had happened in there," the guard said. "I called to him several times but he kept walking without answering. I'm not sure he heard me."

The guard was correct on all counts. Hawkins didn't hear him. He was completely undone by the bomb Mathews dropped. Mathews' whole performance was beyond belief, beyond recovery. Here was the outlaw Fed chief telling the country about the sham of the monetary system and how it's used to draw blood and treasure from everyday working people to feed the power lusts of the politically privileged. *And he was doing the telling from the White House, at the invitation of the president, on national TV!* Reality was supposed to have gates to keep such things from happening.

Surely Mathews knew his death was now guaranteed. No one with so much power and prestige lavished on him is permitted to turn the other way. The very people who had the power to set him up had the power to take him down.  And they would use that power.  It was certain – absolutely certain.

Whistleblowers were to be expected on the lower rungs, but never as high as Mathews.  When a rank-and-file voice screams "foul" then suddenly disappears with little notice in the mainstream media, it's left to conspiracy theory nuts to take up the cause.  And with that label, who's going to believe them?

But Mathews found a way to beat the system.  He positioned himself on the top rung then disappeared first, before anyone could get to him.  His was a guerilla war from the beginning.  Mathews, the antiwar traitor, going to war on a shoestring against the world's greatest power.  It didn't matter that no one considered gold and cutthroat banking a workable solution.  What mattered was the exposure of the system currently in place.  *His* exposure of it – a voice from the sky, an authoritative voice condemning it as a racket, a counterfeiting operation, a fraud financing much of the misery of the past century.

Hawkins arrived at his office almost without realizing it and dropped into his chair.  It was from this chair that he saw Mathews' take-over of Peter Allport's spot from Arlington.  Little wonder he had the *bolas* to walk into the White House tonight.  After Arlington, he no doubt thought he was unstoppable.

Hawkins stood up suddenly, grabbed a genuine marble paper weight from a corner of his expansive desk and flung it across the room.  *"Bastard!"* he blurted out, then followed it with stronger language.  His rage fueled, he cleared his desk, hurling pens, a notebook, two plaques, a desk calendar, a stainless steel letter-opener, a pop-up mirror with a Chinese saying inscribed on the outside ("A man must learn to sail in all winds"), and several mahogany coasters in the same general direction, amalgamating his throws with appropriate invective. Something fell and broke somewhere. He ignored it. He even tried to lift the desk itself, struggling until he purpled. He was about to try heaving his chair until he caught sight of the desk's bottom right drawer.

He dropped the chair and yanked the drawer open. Inside was a white linen hand towel wrapped around itself.

He paused for a moment, panting, then reached for the towel.

Mathews and Levy stayed for a portion of Gage's follow-up speech then slipped out. They moved briskly toward the north side exit. They had completed their mission inside enemy territory and saw no reason to stay longer. They could catch the complete story later on replay.

"*Mathews!*" came a desperate shout from behind. They stopped and turned.

Hawkins came running after them but stopped some ten feet away. He clutched the towel in his left hand. "It's over, Mathews! You lost! You think you've won but you haven't! You appeal to the lowest forms of life because only halfwits will listen to you. Thanks to your little stunt in there, the whole country now knows how vacuous your campaign is. You think because you've got females running around with tattoos of demented dollars on their private parts you're some kind of star. Well, get this – your star only shines over La-la-

land. You don't impress the movers of this world one bit, unless it's with your idiocy."

Two female aides came out from a room behind Hawkins, stopped and stared. "You want to know what winners do?!" he bellowed, taking a step closer. "They build palaces like this on top of chumps like you! That's right! You've got your precious principles – we've got the power and the money! And we get that money and power from you! Try buying a hot dog with your lousy principles sometime! Someone like Gage will always rule because that's what—"

He looked around wildly, caught sight of one of the aides, went over and grabbed her by the arm and shoved her in their direction. She looked scared to death.

"—All of these fools, tell them they're patriotic and they'll gladly keep their mouths shut and fall in line! We can tax them and inflate their flimsy dollars however much we want because they're goddamn idiots! Look at her! *Look* at her! Do you think she knows the first thing about what money is? Do you think she gives a damn? No! No one cares! *No one fricking cares!* That's the way it is, and that's the way it's always going to be! And you know it!" He flung her to one side. She scrambled back to her associate. They looked like they wanted to run but were too caught up with Hawkins' outburst.

"Idiots don't have rights! If they had more sense they'd thank us for sparing them! They couldn't exist without us! They don't want to think – they want to salute someone who'll think for them! You don't understand the first thing about human nature! If you did you wouldn't have to pull all these half-assed stunts to get their attention! You're a loser, gold's a loser, all of your goddamn little piss-pot followers are losers!"

Mathews and Levy started to turn but Hawkins moved closer. "Even your principles are phony! You two are guilty of high treason! You're attempting to overthrow this government! Without the iron hand of government the bastards would kill and rob one another! Admit it! You know it's true! It *is* true, whether you admit it or not! People go around telling each other to have a nice day, but beneath the thin crust they're slime! I've got my place in the world assured because I know them for what they are. You're on the outside running around like a fool because you think there's decency in them. You must've majored in fairy tales! That's the only place you'll find human decency!"

"I find decent people everywhere I turn," Mathews said calmly. He glanced at Levy, adding, "Even in government, much to my surprise. But here's a chance to see who's on your side. Arrest us. Our only guilt is telling the truth as we see it. In today's world, real patriots talk treason."

"Your ability to twist truth is uncanny, Mathews," Hawkins said. "I've never heard anyone like you. At least you're unique."

"Check your history books. I believe a guy named Henry said pretty much the same during our revolutionary days, though much more eloquently."

"Yeah? Well, a guy named Mathews isn't going to start another revolution, no matter how much he tries." He unraveled the towel with a bold sweep of his arm, revealing Gage's Glock 19. He pointed it at them, his hand shaking with fury. "You think we're going to let a couple of stiff-backs ruin a good thing? You blew it, guys. You should've faked it and acted like men, instead of trying to sneak out of here like the cowards you are. The great Preston Mathews, shot like a rabbit running for a hole."

"We'll get what we deserve, I'm sure," Mathews said. They turned and headed for the exit.

"Go ahead, walk away, make it easier for me! You're idiots! *You're traitors! You're arrogant traitors! You're enemies of this government and the people it represents! I'm duly authorized— do you hear me?!—I'm duly authorized—*" He squeezed the trigger, and to Hawkins' dumb surprise the gun clicked.

Mathews and Levy kept walking. Hawkins kept firing, and the gun kept clicking.

Mathews stopped, turned, and looked at the thoroughly vexed Chief of Staff, who suddenly wailed like an animal caught in a trap. Mathews shook his head. "Fiat bullets now? What next?"

## 42

Levy drove Mathews back to the spot where he picked him up. Neither said a word on the way. They got out and began walking towards the tavern. It was raining steadily but they didn't seem to notice. They moved with effort. Their faces looked strained.

"How're you doing?" Mathews asked.

"Mentally computing our life expectancy. What would you say? A couple of weeks?"

"I don't know. I've refused to think that way. The government is no different now than it was an hour ago. The fight is just beginning, and I plan to stay in it as long as I can."

Levy looked at him. "Spoken like a true soldier . . . Right now, I'm numb, though. How about you?"

"I'm too numb to tell."

"Think the TV audience believed us?"

"Some did, I'm sure. Even if they all did, even if they believed our every word, we'd still have major problems. The

enemy is a fulltime aggressor, the people at most a part-time
defender. And the enemy is organized and lethal. The
people—" Mathews came to an abrupt halt. He looked
confused and distressed.

"What's wrong?" Levy asked, stopping a step ahead of
him.

"She means everything to me," Mathews said, with a
visible effort to keep his voice even, "and I betrayed her. It
was only an act, but she didn't know that. I let her down . . ."

"What do you mean?"

Mathews let out a long slow breath. "I couldn't stay
married to her and lead the attack on the Fed. I decided to
divorce her to convince certain parties I was sincere in my
acceptance of the status quo. She never knew why I wanted to
split. I made her think I had changed, that I had come to
believe in the almighty goodness of managed currency. If
someone asked her why we broke up . . . I needed her
animosity to be genuine."

"Lord, man. Are you nuts?"

Mathews turned his face up, to let the rain wash it. "No.
That's the problem."

"I guess you have a right to feel rotten," Levy said. "You
used her . . . you used everyone."

Mathews looked at him. "I did. I became a different
person. I had to talk like Keynesians and Monetarists, but
think like an Austrian. I had to lead two lives. It wore on me.
I *was* nuts. I became a robot."

"No, robots can't be held accountable. People can. You
were an actor. You put on an act for which you were fully

responsible, and you did a good job. Are you telling me you're just now aware of it?"

"In the sense that it's finally hitting me, yes. I've shown the world it takes a liar to promote the truth . . . a cheat to usher in honesty."

"Listen, soldier . . ." Levy took a moment to measure his words. "This is starting to sound like self-pity. I don't think that's the way you want to go out. If what you've done will lead to fewer wars, if young people will greet their future with optimism instead of sacrificing it for lying politicians—"

"—Stop it, okay? Just . . . just stop it."

"No! I've got a grandson still in diapers. I want him to be a free man someday. I want him to be able to ignore the damn government. I don't want him living under some BS decree that says it can do with him whatever it sees fit because a bunch of goddamn politicians and their sponsors got together behind closed doors and cooked up some deals. All right, you feel lousy, go ahead and feel that way, but I'm looking ahead, and if all those stunts you pulled, and that speech you made, and maybe because of what I said today—"

Mathews was trying not to listen. "Do me a favor." He let out a slow breath. "Tell her I apologize. Tell her I don't ask her forgiveness. Make that clear – I don't ask her forgiveness. I can't be forgiven. But for God's sake be sure to tell her I apologize."

Levy was getting worked up. "No, I won't. What the hell's come over you? I'm not going to tell her a damn thing – that's your job. And I'd feel like a complete fool if I tried!

You're going to tell her yourself – in person. Come on, let's go."

"No."

Levy crossed his arms and waited. Mathews reluctantly got his legs moving again. They walked together, nearing the tavern entrance.

"It would be more humane if you just shot me," Mathews said.

"I know."

"You're a bit of a bastard yourself. Maybe she'll disappoint you. Maybe she'll buy me a beer."

They arrived at the door. Levy opened it and turned to Mathews. "I wouldn't count on it, soldier."

They went inside.

The End

Afterward: The Writer is a Thief

When I moved from Buffalo to Atlanta in 1979 and began work for an electric utility, I knew someday I would leave and attempt a writing career. A few weeks into my job I came across a newspaper headline that consisted of the song title, "Gonna Fly Now!" I have long since forgotten the accompanying story, if I even bothered to read it. I cut the headline out and taped it to the inside top of my office trash basket as a reminder. People sometimes lose sight of their goals. I didn't want that to happen to me.

As the years passed, I took the waste basket with me whenever I switched departments or moved to a different building. A thing of beauty it isn't. It's a black clunker, not the least stylish, but it was the most important part of my office baggage.

On a July morning in 1999, as I was leaving downtown headquarters for the last time and about to begin my new career, I had the basket in my arms as I was passing the guard's station in the lobby. It was filled with personal items – pictures of my kids, mostly – as if I were moving to a new office within the company. But the guard knew I was on my way out for keeps and asked me if I was stealing company property. I said, yes, I was. We both laughed, and I continued on out the door.

As I type these words now the trash basket sits on the floor of my home office, the *Rocky* theme song title untouched after 29 years.

Yes, the writer is a thief. But maybe he can be forgiven.

Acknowledgements and recommendations for further reading

I'm intellectually indebted to more people than I could possibly name, but I wish to acknowledge a particularly large debt to the late Murray N. Rothbard and to G. Edward Griffin. Their writings broke down the mysteries and made this book possible.

In addition, I salute the memory of Ayn Rand, whose works stirred me long ago and were the foundation of my decision to "someday" try writing.

I also wish to acknowledge the invaluable services of the Mises Institute in Auburn, Alabama, who have made the works of many free-market economists and social critics available as free downloads on their website, http://www.mises.org/. Through their online store they also sell the works of Rothbard, Ludwig von Mises, Ron Paul, and many other libertarian thinkers.

Readers wishing a more systematic and detailed presentation of the economic issues I've raised in this story might find the following works helpful:

1. Rothbard, Murray N., *What Has Government Done to Our Money?*, Ludwig von Mises Institute, Auburn University, Auburn, Alabama, 1990. A classic primer on how money originated, and how and why government took it over.

2. Rothbard, Murray N., *The Case Against the Fed*, Ludwig von Mises Institute, Auburn University, Auburn, Alabama, 1990. A detailed presentation of the origins of the American central bank and how it functions as our engine of inflation.

3.  Griffin, G. Edward, *The Creature from Jekyll Island: A Second Look at the Federal Reserve*, American Media, Westlake Village, CA, 2002.  A close look at the Fed, who made it, how it works, who it benefits, its connection to our wars, depressions, and our currency meltdown, plus its vital role in the plans of internationalists.

And – be sure to visit the real BRC:
http://www.barbarous-relic.com/

George F. Smith
Lawrenceville, Georgia
January, 2008

1179879

Made in the USA